The Illusionless Man

The Illusionless Man

Fantasies and Meditations

by Allen Wheelis

HARPER COLOPHON BOOKS
Harper & Row, Publishers
New York, Evanston, San Francisco, London

In an abridged form "To Be a God" was published in
Commentary in August, 1963; "The Illusionless Man and the
Visionary Maid" was published in *Commentary* in May,
1964; "Sea Girls" was published in *The Yale Review* in
the summer 1966 issue; "The Signal" was published in
Ramparts in July, 1966.

This book was originally published by W. W. Norton & Company, Inc. and
is here reprinted by arrangement.

First HARPER COLOPHON edition published 1971

STANDARD BOOK NUMBER: 06-090250-7

Fantasies

Meditations

Fantasies

THE ILLUSIONLESS MAN AND THE VISIONARY MAID

ONCE UPON A TIME
THERE WAS A MAN WHO
had no illusions about anything. While still in the crib he had learned that his mother was not always kind; at two he had given up fairies; witches and hobgoblins disappeared from his world at three; at four he knew that rabbits at Easter lay no eggs; and at five on a cold night in December, with a bitter little smile, he said good-bye to Santa Claus. At six when he started school illusions flew from his life like feathers in a windstorm: he discovered that his father was not always brave or even honest, that presidents are little men, that the Queen of England goes to the bathroom like everybody else, and that his first-grade teacher, a pretty round-faced young woman with dimples, did not know everything, as he had thought, but thought only of men and did not in fact know much of anything. At eight he could read, and the printed word was a sorcerer at exorcising illusions—only he knew there were no sorcerers. The abyss of hell disappeared into the even larger abyss into which a clear vision was sweeping his beliefs. Happiness

3

was of course a myth; love a fleeting attachment, a dream of enduring selflessness glued onto the instinct of a rabbit. At twelve he dispatched into the night sky his last unheard prayer. As a young man he realized that the most generous act is self-serving, the most disinterested inquiry serves interest; that lies are told by printed words, even by words carved in stone; that art begins with a small "a" like everything else, and that he could not escape the ruin of value by orchestrating a cry of despair into a song of lasting beauty; for beauty passes and deathless art is quite mortal. Of all those people who lose illusions he lost more than anyone else, taboo and prescription alike; and as everything became permitted nothing was left worth while.

He became a carpenter but could see a house begin to decay in the course of building—perfect pyramid of white sand spreading out irretrievably in the grass, bricks chipping, doors sticking, the first tone of gray appearing on white lumber, the first film of rust on bright nails, the first leaf falling in the shining gutter. He became then a termite inspector, spent his days crawling in darkness under old houses; he lived in a basement room and never raised the blinds, ate canned beans and frozen television dinners, let his hair grow and his beard. On Sundays he walked in the park, threw bread to the ducks—dry French bread, stone-hard, would stamp on it with his heel, gather up the pieces, and walk along the pond, throwing it out to the avid ducks paddling after him, thinking glumly that they would be just as hungry again tomorrow. His name was Henry.

One day in the park he met a girl who believed in everything. In the forest she still glimpsed fairies, heard them whisper; bunnies hopped for her at Easter, laid brilliant eggs; at Christmas hoofbeats shook the roof. She was disillusioned at times and would flounder, gasp desperately, like a fish in sand, but not for long; would quickly, sometimes instantly, find something new, and actually never gave up any illusion but would lay it aside when necessary, forget it, and whenever it was needed back it would come. Her name was Lorabelle, and when she saw a bearded young man in the park, alone among couples, stamping on the hard bread, tossing it irritably to the quacking ducks, she exploded into illusions about him like a Roman candle over a desert.

"You are a great and good man," she said.

"I'm petty and self-absorbed," he said.

"You're terribly unhappy."

"I'm morose . . . probably like it that way."

"You have suffered a great deal," she said. "I see it in your face."

"I've been diligent only in self-pity," he said, "have turned away from everything difficult, and what you see is the scars of old acne shining through my beard; I could never give up chocolate and nuts."

"You're very wise," she said.

"No, but intelligent."

They talked about love, beauty, feeling, value, love, life, work, death—and always she came back to love. They argued about everything, differed on everything, agreed on

5

nothing, and so she fell in love with him. "This partakes of the infinite," she said.

But he, being an illusionless man, was only fond of her. "It partaketh mainly," he said, "of body chemistry," and passed his hand over her roundest curve.

"We have a unique affinity," she said. "You're the only man in the world for me."

"We fit quite nicely," he said. "You are one of no more than five or six girls in the county for me."

"It's a miracle we met," she said.

"I just happened to be feeding the ducks."

"No, no, no, not chance; I couldn't feel this way about anybody else."

"If you'd come down the other side of the hill," he said, "you'd be feeling this way right now about somebody else. And if I had fed squirrels instead of ducks I'd be playing with somebody else's curves."

"You're my dearest darling squirrel," she said, "and most of all you're my silly fuzzy duck, and I don't know why I bother to love you—why are you such a fool? who dropped you on your head?—come to bed!" On such a note of logic, always, their arguments ended.

She wanted a wedding in church with a dress of white Alençon lace over cream satin, bridesmaids in pink, organ music, and lots of people to weep and be happy and throw rice. "You'll be so handsome in a morning coat," she said, brushing cobwebs from his shoulders, "oh and striped pants, too, and a gray silk cravat, and a white carnation. You'll be divine."

"I'd look a proper fool," he said, "and I'm damned if I'll do it."

"Oh please! It's only once."

"Once a fool, voluntarily, is too often."

"It's a sacrament."

"It's a barbarism."

"Symbols are important."

"Then let's stand by the Washington Monument," he said, "and be honest about it."

"You make fun," she said, "but it's a holy ceremony, a solemn exchange of vows before man and God."

"God won't be there, honey; the women will be weeping for their own lost youth and innocence, the men wanting to have you in bed; and the priest standing slightly above us will be looking down your cleavage as his mouth goes dry; and the whole thing will be a primitive and preposterous attempt to invest copulation with dignity and permanence, to enforce responsibility for children by the authority of a myth no longer credible even to a child."

So . . . they were married in church: his hands were wet and his knees shook, he frowned and quaked; but looked divine, she said, in morning coat and striped pants; and she was serene and beautiful in Alençon lace; the organ pealed, weeping women watched with joy, vows were said, rice thrown, and then they were alone on the back seat of a taxi, her red lips seeking his, murmuring, "I'm so happy, darling, so terribly happy. Now we'll be together always."

"In our community," he said, "and for our age and economic bracket, we have a 47.3% chance of staying together

7

for twenty years."

She found for them a white house on a hill in a field of
orange poppies and white daisies, with three tall maple
trees. There they lived in sunlight and wind, and she began to fill their life with fragile feminine deceptions,
worked tirelessly at them, and always there was something
new. She concealed the monotony of eating by variety,
never two meals the same, one morning French toast in the
shape of their house, the next a boiled egg with smiling
painted face and a tiny straw hat; cut flowers on the table,
color and sweetness blooming from a Dutch vase, as if unrelated to manure; Italian posters on the wall as if they
had traveled; starched white curtains at the windows, as if
made of a brocade too rich and heavy to bend; morning
glories covering the outhouse with royal purple. When he
came home at night she would brush the cobwebs from his
hair, make him bathe and shave and dress—to appear as if
he had not worked in dirt. She made wonderful sauces,
could cook anything to taste like something else, created a
sense of purity by the whiteness of tablecloth, of delicacy by
the thinness of crystal, would surround a steak with parsley
as if it were not flesh but the bloom of a garden, supported
her illusions with candlelight and fine wine, and smiled at
him across the table with lips redder than real. In the bedroom candlelight again, and yet another nightgown to sug-
gest a mysterious woman of unknown delights, and a heavy
perfume, as if not sweat but sweetness came from her
pores.

Being an illusionless man, he knew that he liked these

elegant mirages, found them pleasant, that it was good to sleep with her fine curves under his hand, her sweet smells in his nose, that he slept better now than when he lived alone. He became less gloomy, but not much.

One Sunday afternoon, walking hand in hand in sunshine through the poppies and daisies, he noticed her lips moving. "What are you saying?" he said.

"Do you love me?"

"I'm fond of you," he said; "love is an illusion."

"Is there anybody else? I'm terribly jealous."

"Jealousy is the illusion of complete possession."

"Do other women attract you?"

"Yes."

"Some men are not like that."

"Some men are liars," he said.

"Oh . . ."

". . . Don't cry! I won't leave you."

"How can I be sure?"

"I wouldn't hurt you."

She became pregnant, bought baby clothes, tried out names, was always singing. "Please be happy," she said.

"By 1980 the world population will . . ."

"Oh be quiet!" she said.

She prepared a room for the baby, hung curtains, bought a crib, read books, became apprehensive. "Will he be all right? What do you think? Will he be a good baby? He doesn't have to be pretty, you know, that's not so important, but I'd like him to be intelligent. And will he have two eyes and the right number of fingers and toes? I

9

want him to have everything he needs and nothing too much. What do you think?"

"Some minor congenital aberrations are inevitable," he said; "the major malformations are less. . . ."

"Don't say such things," she said. "Why do you scare me?"

"I was just . . ."

"Oh . . . and will I know what to do?" she said, ". . . how to take care of him? What do you think? Will I be any good at it?"

One night he felt her lips moving in his hair. "Praying?" he said. "Yes." "What did you ask?" "That someday you will say you love me."

She felt weak, became sick; in bed she looked pale and scared. "Will the baby be all right?" she said. "Don't ever leave me. What are you thinking? Tell me." She began to bleed, was terrified, lay very still, but lost the baby anyway.

She was depressed then, her face motionless and dark. "I lost it because you don't love me," she said.

"There is no established correlation," he said, "between the alleged state of love, or lack of it, and the incidence of miscarriage."

"I'm not wanting statistics," she screamed.

"What then?"

"Nothing. Everything. It's not enough . . . just being 'fond.' I hate fondness. What's the matter with you? It wouldn't have happened . . . I want to be loved!"

"You're being hysterical," he said, "and you're not finishing your sentences."

Suddenly, all at once, she looked at him with a level detached gaze and did not like what she saw. "You were right," she said, "you *are* petty and self-absorbed. What's worse, you have a legal mind, and there's no poetry in you. You don't give me anything, don't even love me, you're *dull*. You were stuck in a hole in the ground when I found you, and if I hadn't pulled you out you'd be there still. There's no life in you. I give you everything, and it's not enough, doesn't make any difference. You can't wait to die, want to bury yourself now and me with you. Well I'm not ready yet, and I'm not going to put up with it any longer, and now I'm through with you, and I want a divorce."

"You've lost your illusions about me," he said, "but not the having of illusions . . ."

"While you," she said, "have lost your illusions about everything and can't get over being sore about it."

". . . they'll focus on someone else . . ."

"Oh I hope so!" she said; "I can hardly wait."

". . . you waste experience."

"And you waste *life!*"

He wouldn't give her a divorce, but that didn't matter; for she couldn't bear the thought of his moving back to that basement, and anyway, she told herself, he had to have someone to look after him; so they lived together still, and she cooked for him when she was home and mended his clothes and darned his socks, and when he asked why, she said, with sweet revenge, "Because I'm fond of you, that's all. Just fond."

11

She got a job with a theater, typed scripts and programs, worked nights in the box office, let her hair grow into a long silken curtain curled up at the bottom below her shoulders, wore loose chiffon blouses with clown sleeves, trailed filmy scarves from her neck, and fell in love with an actor named Cyrus Anthony de Maronodeck. Her *a*s broadened, and she affected a way of turning her head with so sudden a movement that it could not go unnoticed; no longer did she walk in or out of rooms, she strode. Again she demanded a divorce, and when Henry refused she taunted him: "Cyrus is so *interesting!*" she said, "makes everything an adventure, concentrates energy and passion into a moment until it glows!" she struck a pose: " 'When I die,' he says, 'I may be dead for a long time, but while I'm here I'll live it to the hilt.' "

"A philosopher, too," Henry said.

One Sunday night Cyrus borrowed a thousand dollars from Lorabelle for his sick mother; and the following day it transpired that he had borrowed also the weekend receipts from the box office and had taken his leave of the company. For several days Lorabelle wouldn't believe it, waited for word from him, bit her fingernails—until he was apprehended in Larado crossing the border with a blond.

She worked next in a brokerage house operating an enormous and very intelligent machine which tapped and hummed and whirred and rotated, sent its carriage hopping up and down and side to side, performed seventeen mathematical calculations without ever a mistake, took pictures of everything, and had illusions about nothing—

but Lorabelle did, and presently fell in love with her boss, Mr. Alexander Orwell Mittelby, a sixty year old man who loved her with a great passion, she told Henry, but who was married and unfortunately could not get a divorce because his wife was a schizophrenic, had a private nurse in constant attendance; the shock of divorce, Mr. Mittelby had said, would kill her.

"Alex is unique," Lorabelle told Henry, "simply not like the rest of us . . . not at all. He has no interest in himself, has grown beyond that. I've never met a man so mature, so genuinely wise. 'All my personal goals lie in the past,' he told me; 'the only thing left is to seek the common good.' He has no patience with personal problems, complexes . . . that sort of thing . . . sees the romantic protest for what it is: adolescent complaining. Oh Henry, I wish you could know him. He faces life with so much courage—such a gallant, careless courage. 'Despair is a luxury,' he says, 'the flight of a frightened intelligence, and I can't afford it.' "

Lorabelle wore short tight skirts, high, needlelike heels, jeweled glasses, and her hair bouffant; she read the *Wall Street Journal* and *Barron's Weekly,* studied the new tax legislation, spoke out for *laissez faire* in discussion groups, and at an Anti-World-Federalist dinner chanced to meet Mrs. Mittelby who was not schizophrenic at all but a plain, shrewd woman with a wrinkled face, gray hair, and a very sharp tongue. Lorabelle stared at her with deepening shock. "My husband's secretaries," Mrs. Mittelby said, "always seem stunned by my sanity . . . then seek other employment."

In her depression Lorabelle turned away from people, rented a cabin on an island, left Henry to look after himself, came home only on weekends, spent her days walking on deserted beaches, her nights alone writing an autobiographical novel by lamplight. "It's really a kind of self-analysis," she said, "but maybe I can make it beautiful, make it sing."

After a few months she fell in love with a fisherman. "His name is Jim," she said to Henry. "That's all, just Jim. And he's like his name, exactly: simple, strong, uncomplicated. I wish you could know each other."

"Bring him to dinner!" Henry shouted. "Let him live here! Give him my clothes, my bed!"

"Don't be angry. You'd like him; you couldn't help it. He's so kind, so gentle, so much a part of the elements: in his eyes the wind and the ocean—you can see them!—in his hand the strength, the toughness . . . the grip on the helm in a storm, in his bearing the straightness of the tall pointed firs, in his character the solid rock of the coast."

"If he had a foundation," Henry said, "he'd be a house with a swimming pool."

Lorabelle cut her hair short, wore boots and a sou'wester, scanned the sky for weather signs, studied navigation charts, hung a tide table on the wall. "I want a divorce," she said. "No." "Why? You don't love me." "To protect you from your own bad judgment. You'd be married six times before you were forty if you were free." "Then I'll run away with him," she said.

And she would have, but the sheriff got there first, arrested Jim for bigamy: plain Jim had three last names and a wife with each, and while he sat in jail the three of them squabbled for the fishing boat, which was all he owned.

Lorabelle gave up the cabin, burned her manuscript, and moved back home; wept and wailed and could not be consoled. "There's something wrong with *my* sanity," she said. "I can't do it myself. I'd better see a psychoanalyst."

"You'll get a whopping transference," Henry said.

She went to a Dr. Milton Tugwell, took to analysis with great facility, worked quickly through her depression, went four times a week, and wished it were more. "I'm so terribly lucky," she said to Henry. "There are so many analysts, you know—good, bad, indifferent—I had no way of knowing . . . and he turns out to be the *one* analyst for me. No one else would be right."

"It really is a kind of miracle, isn't it?" Henry said.

"No, really! I mean it. There's a special affinity between us. I felt it the very first session. We speak the same language; sometimes he knows what I'm thinking before I say it—sometimes even before I know I'm thinking it. It's amazing. And he has the most astonishing memory, remembers *everything*. And the way—Oh, Henry! if you could only know him, hear him talk!—the way he fits these things together! things you'd never realize were connected. . . ."

Dr. Tugwell made many excellent interpretations: Lorabelle learned about her orality, anality, penis envy, oedipus complex, and, as a kind of bonus, had many insights also into Henry and shared them with him, surprised at his lack of responsiveness.

One night at the theater she saw Dr. Tugwell in the company of a tall, gray-haired woman with a hard face. His wife, Lorabelle thought, and something clicked for her, an insight all her own: *Dr. Tugwell was unhappy with this woman.* So this was the source of that sad note in his voice. He deserved better. Lorabelle wanted to make him happy, as a woman; and she could, she knew she could. She looked narrowly at Mrs. Tugwell.

Then it occurred to her (the analysis must be taking effect, she thought; this was her second insight in an hour) that Dr. Tugwell might have some feeling of this sort for her, and the more she thought about it the more obvious it became: the warmth of his greeting, clearly more than professional; the happy loving way he smiled at her; the little things about her he held in his mind, as if deliberately committing her whole life to memory; the caressing tone of that gentle voice floating out over her on the couch. How could she have failed so long to recognize it?

When in her next hour she talked of these matters Dr. Tugwell said nothing except "What comes to mind about that?" and she was disappointed, then realized that he could not speak, that he was the prisoner of a professional commitment which required him to stifle his feeling for her. She walked in the meadow on the hill in sunshine and knew in her heart what must be hidden in his; and someday, she thought, when the analysis was over maybe he would get a divorce and Henry would give her a divorce, and she and Dr. Tugwell would meet on a different basis. She picked a daisy, pulled the petals, and it came out right. Softly she tried his name on her lips, "Milton, darling," and blushed, "sweetest Milt, . . . honey," felt him walk beside her, his hand slip around her waist, heard his deep beloved voice begin, "Lorabelle, there is something I must tell you. . . ."

The analysis lasted longer than any of her affairs, perhaps because, paying for her sessions, she valued them more than meetings with lovers, or perhaps because her illusions did not encounter anything hard enough in Dr. Tugwell's silence to cause breakage; but after five years Henry came to the end of his resources and tolerance, said he would pay for no more sessions. This proved him cruel and unfeeling, Lorabelle thought, and reported it triumphantly to Dr. Tugwell who, strangely, regarded it as reasonable.

Lorabelle wept through the last hour, tears making lakes in her ears, overflowing on the pillow, dripping from her chin as she stood up, shaking, to face him, her voice quavering as she thanked him for the changes in her, breaking as she said good-bye. Yet at that very moment she had the comfort of a secret vision: now that she was no longer his patient he was free to become her lover. But days passed, and he didn't call, weeks and the vision was shaken, a month and she was desolate. She went back to see him; and this time, sitting in a chair before him, feeling oddly dislocated, really did *see* him. There along the wall was the green couch on which she had lain for so many hours, from which she had looked up at the blank ceiling, had raved, rambled, complained, and wept; and there—shrinking back slightly from the violence of her disappointment—was the man of her dreams who had listened, out of sight, behind the couch: dark suit of expensive cloth and cut, perfectly pressed, dark tie, silk shirt with white-on-white design, high cordovan sheen on calf-skin loafers, shell-rimmed glasses flashing a nervous glare. There was strain in his voice, she thought; he used jargon, was more detached than he need have been: a continuing transference problem, he said . . . not infrequent . . . might require further analysis . . . unresolved father attachment . . . he had committed her hours . . . could do nothing now . . . sorry . . . perhaps later . . . call him in three months.

For weeks Lorabelle stayed home in deep silent gloom, wouldn't eat, wouldn't dress; but bounced back finally, as she always did, got a job selling tickets at a carousel, and there met Adelbert Bassew, big game hunter—"What a man!" she exclaimed to Henry; "six feet six, all fire and brawn. Imagine!"—who asked her on a safari. And so it continued through the days and weeks of their lives, year after year: Catholic church, Christian Science, yoga; Al, Bob, and Peter; Paris, Rome, and Nairobi; technocracy, mysticism, hypnotism; short hair, long hair, and wig; and whenever she would say, in that rapturous tone of hers, "I realize now . . ." Henry would know she had abandoned one illusion and was already firmly entrapped by the next. They became poor on her pursuits, lived in a basement;

her illusions became sillier, shabbier, until finally she was sending in box-tops from cereal packages. Crow's feet appeared around her eyes, white hair among the gold; her skin became dry and papery. But as she got older something about her stayed young: the spinging up of hope, the intoxicating energy, the creation of a new dream from the ruin of the old. From the despair of disillusion always she would find her way back: back to a bell-like laughter with the rising note of an unfinished story, to a lilt of voice like the leap of water before rapids, to a wild dancing grace of legs and hips like a horse before a jump, to the happy eyes so easily wet with sympathy or love.

But these same years made Henry older than his actual age, more withdrawn, bitter, morose; his face haggard, lined; his hair gray. Every day he got up and went to work, but did nothing else—would not read a book or walk in the park or listen to music. In the evenings he would drink; but gin nourished no illusion, brought no pleasure, only numbness and finally sleep. Lorabelle felt anger and pity and contempt, all at the same time, and would rail at him. "Just look at yourself: drunk, dirty, head hanging like a sick cat . . . How can you stand yourself? What are you trying to do? Make me feel guilty . . . Well I don't. Playing the martyr? Is that it? What's the matter with you? Why don't you find someone else if you're so unhappy with me?"

Henry would shrug, thinking there are no happy marriages, and it would be no different with anyone else; but sometimes, far at the back of his unhappy mind, he would

19

come upon the truth: he stayed with her because, with all her witless pursuit of illusions, she nevertheless stirred him—like the wren, trapped under a house, that had flown in his face: he had caught it in his hand, felt the terrified struggle, the concentration of heat, the tremulo of heartbeat too faint and fast to count. Lorabelle brought him no comfort; but, holding her, he felt life and would not give it up. And sometimes in the midst of her railings Lorabelle would know that she stayed with Henry—not simply, as she said, because he wouldn't give her a divorce—but because he was a rock and she leaned on him.

But even rocks may crumble, and one Monday morning Henry did not move when the alarm went off; he lay still, eyes open, looking at the empty face of the clock, thinking numbly of millions of termites burrowing in wood who would suffer no further interference from him.

He stayed in bed most of the day, ate little, drank much, said nothing. The next day was the same, and the next, and so all week; and on Friday it occurred to Lorabelle that—Henry having apparently retired from business—she must earn the living. After her morning coffee, therefore, she sat down at her desk to compose the fourth line of a jingle about soap flakes; first prize would bring a thousand dollars. Next she invented a hatpin that could neither fall out of a hat nor prick a finger; drew a careful sketch of the device and addressed it to the Patent Office; this might make a fortune, she thought. Then she collected all her green stamps: not many, she mused, but enough for a present for Henry. She prepared his lunch on a tray, found him lying in bed staring at the ceiling; he would say nothing and would not eat. She put on her best dress, arranged flowers by his bed, and kissed him on the nose. "I'll be back soon," she said.

It was a beautiful day, the sun shining, wind moving here and there among the trees like playful strokes of a great invisible brush. "I know he will be all right," she said to herself and posted her jingle and her invention, saying a little prayer for each. She went then to a fortune-teller, an old West Indian woman, who told her that someone dear to her was ill and would die. Lorabelle was shocked and left immediately, bought three sweepstakes tickets in Henry's name to fight the prediction, said another prayer, went on to the supply house, and got a pipe and slippers for her green stamps. For a dollar she bought jonquils—because they were pretty and would make him happy—then counted her money. With the two dollars that were left she bought a steak to tempt his appetite.

At home she found him in pyjamas sitting at the table drinking gin. "Oh, sweetheart!" she said, "you break my heart . . . I won't have it, I just won't have it . . . you understand? Cheer up now. I've got presents for you." She put the pipe in his hand, brought tobacco, put the slippers on his bare feet—"There! You see? Aren't they nice? And so warm. A perfect fit! You like them?"—but he said nothing. She began to sing, trying not to cry, then broke off: "Oh, and I have something else . . . another wonderful surprise, you'll see. Now don't come in the kitchen," she added, unnecessarily. She broiled the steak, put it on a heated plate, garnished it with water cress, put jonquils on the tray, a chef's cap on her head, lighted candles, and brought it in singing the Triumphal March from *Aïda,* placed it before him with a flourish and a sweeping low bow. He turned away. "Oh, please, do eat it," she cried; "I got it just for you. It's delicious, you'll see! Try it. Would be so good for you."

"Where's the gin?" he said.

"Don't drink any more; you'll get sick. I'm so worried. Eat now. You'll feel better, I know you will, really, . . . I just know it. Here, let me feed you."

She cut a bit of steak, waved it under his nose, held it to his mouth, touched his lips; he knocked it away, the fork clattering to the floor, the morsel skittering into a corner. She picked them up, took away the tray. In the kitchen she threw the fork at the calendar, kicked the garbage can, wept, then she composed herself and went back, humming, to the living room; Henry had not moved. Lorabelle put up a card table, took newspaper clippings from her purse, spread out maps of the city: she was working on a treasure hunt. Only three clues had been published, and already she had an idea where the treasure might be. The first prize was five thousand dollars; tomorrow she would take a shovel and go digging.

"Where's the gin?" Henry said.

"There isn't any more, sweetheart. And a good thing because you've had too much. You're drunk; you're ruining your health."

"Give me some money," he said tonelessly.

"We haven't any."

He got up, walked unsteadily to the table where she was sitting, opened her purse and took out her wallet. A few coins fell to the table, rolled on the floor; there were no bills. He turned her handbag upside down: an astrology chart tumbled out, then a Christian Science booklet, a handbill from the Watchtower Society, "Palmistry in Six Easy Lessons," dozens of old sweepstakes tickets and the three new ones, "Love and the Mystic Union," fortunes from Chinese cookies (one of which, saying "He loves you," she snatched away from him), a silver rosary, a daily discipline from the Rosicrucians, the announcement of a book titled *Secret Power from the Unconscious through Hypnosis*—but no money. He shook the bag furiously and threw it in a corner, surveyed the litter before him with unblinking bloodshot eyes, his face expressionless. "Stupid fool!" he said thickly. "Purse full of illusions . . . suitcase full of illusions . . . whole god damned lousy life full of illusions . . ." He turned away, stumbled back to the table, put the empty gin bottle to his mouth, turned it over his head, broke it on the hearth.

"Oh, my dear," Lorabelle cried, her eyes wet, "you keep waiting for the real thing, but this is all there is." He turned ponderously, facing her, eyes like marble; she came to him. "These are the days . . . and nights . . . of our years and they're passing—look at us! we're getting old—and what else is there?"

"Bitch!"

She faltered, raising her arm, but recovered and went on to touch the side of his head where the hair was gray. "Do please come back to life; I don't want you to die; I'd be so lonely. I'd forget all the bad times and remember all the wonderful things . . . where have they gone? . . . you feeding the ducks, stamping on the bread—so sweet you were!"

"Get out."

The gray stonelike face above her did not move, not even the eyes. A death mask, she thought; the fortune-teller was right. "Oh my dear! I feel so sad." She cried, lowered her head; with a convulsive movement caught his hand, pressed it to her heart. "It hurts so," she said. "For years you've been cutting yourself off . . . more and more. I'm the only one still holding you, and now you're drifting away. Don't die, sweetheart, let me help you, hold on to me!"

He freed his hand and hit her in the face, sent her crashing into the wall, started after her, thinking, Where's that broken bottle? realized with a sense of strangeness that he wanted to kill her . . . paused. She stood looking at him, tears running down her face, then left the room. He turned back to the table, sat heavily, observed the hand that had hit her; the fingers felt numb. Before him on the table was the hatpin she had worked with that morning: long sharp pin, black plastic ball at one end, at the other an odd device of safety pins and scotch tape. "Illusion!" he said, grabbing it up in clenched fist and driving it deep into the table; the plastic ball broke, the base of the pin went through his hand, stuck out three inches on top. There was no blood. His hand hung there in midair, quivering slightly, like an insect pinned to a card. He moved his fingers: a white crab without a shell, he thought, impaled on a boy's stick. Blood appeared around the pin; the feeling of numbness crept up his arm; he wanted a drink, didn't want to die yet, wasn't ready. Numbness came now to the other arm. He began tugging at the pin, ten cold crab's legs fumbling around a spike.

The next morning he shaved, got dressed, and ate breakfast. He felt restless, wanted to do something but didn't know what. "Will you go for a walk with me?" he said. Lorabelle was tired, her eyes red, hadn't slept, but was never without hope. "Yes," she said.

They walked by rivers, over bridges, through forests, sat in dry grass, and watched a tiny squirrel at the tip of a branch in a fir tree; walked through meadows, by cliffs, over dunes, along the beach, saw two sea stars in a tide pool waving their arms at each other; walked on streets, between high buildings, through crowds, watched a little girl feeding pigeons by a fountain. Lorabelle was silent and dejected, her hair scraggly, her shoulders stooped. Something was moving inside Henry, pressing him; he wanted to say something but didn't know what.

That evening as they sat together in their basement room, silent and unhappy, the phone rang. Henry, having known since childhood that a telephone ring means re-

quests, burdens, and obligations, did not move; and for the
first time Lorabelle—to whom the same sound meant love,
opportunity, adventure—did not answer. Henry looked up,
saw that she was exhausted: "Let it ring," he said. She
nodded, but couldn't bear the sense of someone calling un-
heeded, began to hope as she walked, walked faster as she
hoped, was soon running lest she be too late, and a few
moments later was exclaiming in astonishment and joy:
"What? . . . No! . . . Really? Yes! yes! oh yes, he's right
here. . . . No, I have it. . . . So much! That's wonderful!
Marvelous!" then flung herself in Henry's arms, weeping,
laughing, "You've won the Irish Sweepstakes! $137,000!
Can you imagine! My God . . . !"

Henry was pleased, but confused and vaguely disturbed;
said it was hers not his, since she had bought the ticket.
"No, no," she said, "I bought it in your name, and it's
yours and I'm so happy I could cry. . . ." She wiped her
tears. "You need it, darling, more than I . . . because I've
always known about miracles but you haven't known, but
now maybe you will, a little, and I'm so glad it happened
for you. Isn't it marvelous?"

"It won't be much after taxes."

"Oh, but still a lot," she said, "a very great deal. Just
think . . . ! We'll go to Paris and live in the Ritz, and
you'll have a dark blue suit and a gray silk tie and cufflinks
of lapis and maybe a black stick with a little silver. You'll
stand very straight and swing the stick lightly, back and
forth, as we stroll on the Boulevard St. Germain and the
Rue St. Honoré, and I'll be so proud." She sat on his lap,

eyes glistening, hugged him, kissed the gray hair by his ear. "Then we'll get a Citroën and drive down the Loire and come finally to beautiful sand and water. Oh, and Monte Carlo! We'll stand around the casino watching the Texas oilmen and the pretty girls and the diamond bracelets; we'll hold hands and look on at roulette and moisten our lips and be like poor cautious tourists, and nobody will know we're rich. Then you'll toss out a ten thousand dollar bill: 'Red,' you'll say. That's all, just that: 'Red,' in a quiet voice, and people will fall silent and stare, and the croupier's hand will tremble, and the wheel will spin and, oh! . . . it won't matter whether it's red or black because it's just money either way, not love, and we'll go on to Rome and rent a villa, and when . . ."

"We're broke," he said, "long before Rome. In Genoa we couldn't pay the hotel bill. Remember? Had to sell your jewels . . . and my walking stick."

"Oh no!" she said, "there you go, already sad. . . . Then we remembered the *other* bank account—how could you forget?—found we had plenty of money. . . . We go on to Rome, rent a villa, and in the evening sit on the terrace holding hands, flowers blooming all around us, and to the west on the crest of a hill seven cypress trees in a row, an orange sun sinking between the black trunks, the whole sky a brilliant golden drum; and you'll feel a throbbing of your heart and a kind of singing rapture, and you'll press my hand and say, 'I love you.' "

Henry was touched by her fantasy and felt some lightness of heart: it would be nice to have some money, he thought—how incredible!—and maybe they really would enjoy a trip. That night they slept in each other's arms and the next day the windfall was gone: it had been a mistake, the officials were terribly sorry, it was another man with the same name and almost the same telephone number, who owned a candy store and had five children, weighed three hundred pounds, and was pictured in the newspaper with his family, seven round beaming faces. Lorabelle was in despair, but Henry was tranquil, still felt that lightness of heart. He comforted Lorabelle and stroked her finally to sleep in the evening, her wet face on his shoulder. It was an illusion, he thought, and for a while I believed it, and yet—curious thing—it has left some sweetness. Throughout the night he marveled about this—could it be that he had won something after all?—and the next day, crawling under the rotting mansion of a long-dead actor, he looked a termite in the eye and decided to build a house.

He bought land by the sea and built on a cliff by a great madrona tree that grew out horizontally from the rock, a shimmering cloud of red and green; built with massive A-frames, bolted together, stressed, braced, anchored in concrete to withstand five-hundred-mile winds, a house— in the best illusory style, he thought wryly—to last forever. But the cliff crumbled one night in a storm during a twenty-four foot tide; Lorabelle and Henry stood hand in hand in the rain and lightning, deafened by crashing surf and thunder, as the house fell slowly into the sea while the great madrona remained, anchored in nothing but dreams. They went then to live in an apartment, and Henry worked as a carpenter, built houses for other people, began planning another house of his own.

One evening after dinner Henry was sitting at the table, smoking a pipe, working on blueprints; across the room Lorabelle, at her desk, bent over a "Who Am I?" contest. ("We might win $3,500," she had said; "just think of it! Wouldn't that be marvelous? Oh the things we will do . . . !") She was humming now, a waltz from *Die Fledermaus*. Henry looked up, observed the happy face bent to the illusory task, the golden hair streaked with gray falling across her cheek, the wrinkles of laughter now indelible around her eyes, the putting of pencil to mouth like a child, puzzled . . . laid down his pipe. "I love you, Lorabelle," he said. She looked up, startled: "What . . . did you say?" "I love you," he said. She blushed, started to rise, the pencil falling from her hand: "But, . . . but, . . . you said it was an illusion." It is, he thought, because love claims the future and can't hold it; but claims also the present, and we have that. Not wanting to confuse her or start an argument, he said only, "I love you anyway." She ran to him, weeping with joy, "Oh, Henry, I'm so happy, so terribly happy! This is all we lacked . . . all we'll ever need." He took her and the moment in his arms, kissed her, and said nothing.

He built a house on a plateau in a sheltered valley, protected from wind and water; blasted a gigantic hole in solid granite, floated the house on a bubble of pure mercury for earthquakes, built walls of reënforced concrete seven feet thick, doors and cabinets of stainless steel, pipes and lightning rods of copper, roof of inch-thick slate. "Oh, Henry, I'm so proud!" Lorabelle said. "You're a great builder. I'd like to see what could happen to this house." "You'll see," Henry said darkly. It cost a fortune, and they couldn't meet the payments; the bank took it over, sold it to a university as a seismograph station; Henry and Lorabelle moved to an attic in the city.

One afternoon Lorabelle came home in a rapturous mood. "Oh, Henry, I've met the most wonderful man!" "Sorry to hear that," Henry said. "Oh no!" Lorabelle exclaimed, "you'd like him . . . really. There's a kind spiritual quality, . . . he's a graduate student of Far Eastern studies and, . . . you know, sort of a mystic himself . . . name is Semelrad Apfelbaum . . . gives seminars on Buddhism." "Sounds like the real thing all right," Henry said bitterly.

That evening after dinner Lorabelle put on a dress of black chiffon, a flowing lavender scarf, a gold chain around her neck, a sapphire on her finger, perfume in her hair. "Where are you going?" Henry said. "To meet Semelrad," she said; "he's so wonderfully kind, and so generous . . . is going to tutor me privately till I catch up with the class." "You're not going anywhere," Henry said. "I'm not a child, Henry," Lorabelle said with dignity. "But you *are*—precisely," Henry said. Lorabelle reminded him that theirs was a relationship of equality, with the same rights, that she must live her own life, make her own decisions, her own mistakes if need be; and when this failed to convince him she tossed back her head, affected great hauteur, and marched out of the room. Henry caught her at the door, turned her over his knee, applied the flat of his hand to the bottom of his delight; and it was perhaps that same night —for she did not go out—that Lorabelle got pregnant, and this time didn't lose it: the baby was born on Christmas, blue eyes and golden hair, and they named her Noel.

Henry built a house of solid brick in a meadow of sage and thyme, and there Noel played with flowers and crickets and butterflies and field mice. Most of the time she was a joy to her parents, and some of the time—when she was sick or unkind—she was a sorrow. Lorabelle loved the brick house, painted walls, hung pictures, and polished floors; on hands and knees with a bonnet on her head she dug in the earth and planted flowers, looked up at Henry through a wisp of hair with a happy smile; "We'll never move again," she said. But one day the state sent them away and took over their house to build a freeway. The steel ball crashed through the brick walls, bulldozers sheared away the flower beds, the great shovels swung in, and the house was gone. Henry and Lorabelle and Noel moved back to the city, lived in a tiny flat under a water tank that dripped continuously on the roof and sounded like rain.

Henry and Lorabelle loved each other most of the time, tried to love each other all the time, to create a pure bond, but could not. It was marred by the viciousness, shocking to them, with which they hurt each other. Out of nothing they would create fights, would yell at each other, hate, withdraw finally in bitter silent armistice; then, after a few hours, or sometimes a few days, would come together again, with some final slashes and skirmishes, and try to work things out—to explain, protest, forgive, understand, forget, and above all to compromise. It was a terribly painful and always uncertain process; and even while it was underway Henry would think bleakly, It won't last, will never last; we'll get through this one maybe, probably, then all will be well for a while—a few hours, days, weeks if we're lucky—then another fight over something—what? —not possible to know or predict, and certainly not to prevent, . . . and then all this to go through again; and beyond that still another fight looming in the mist ahead, coming closer, . . . and so on without end. But even while thinking these things he still would try to work through the current trouble because, as he would say, "There isn't anything else." And sometimes there occurred to him, uneasily, beyond all this gloomy reflection, an even more sinister thought: that their fights were not only unavoidable but also, perhaps, necessary; for their passages of greatest tenderness followed hard upon their times of greatest bitterness, as if love could be renewed only by gusts of destruction.

Nor could Henry ever build a house that would last forever, no more than anyone else; but he built one finally that lasted quite a while, a white house on a hill with lilac and laurel and three tall trees, a maple, a cedar, and a hemlock. It was an ordinary house of ordinary wood, and the termites caused some trouble, and always it needed painting or a new roof or a faucet dripped or something else needed fixing, and he grew old and gray and finally quite stooped doing these things, but that was all right, he knew, because there wasn't anything else.

Noel grew up in this house—a dreamy, soft-spoken girl, becoming more and more beautiful—wore her long hair in pigtails, practiced the piano, sang in a high, true voice, played in the meadow, caught butterflies among the lilac. At nineteen she fell in love with Falbuck Wheeling who wore a tattered brown leather jacket and roared in on a heavy motorcycle dispelling peace and birds and butterflies, bringing noise and fumes and a misery Henry felt but could not define. Falbuck had a hard bitter face, said little, would sit at the kitchen table sullen and uncomfortable, and Henry could never get him into conversation because whatever the subject—literature, government, justice— Falbuck would sit staring at him, silent and disbelieving, until finally with a few labored and nasty words he would assert some rottenness behind the façade; then, as if exhausted by this excursion into communication, he would get up, taking Noel as if he owned her, and roar away. Noel spent her days with him, and soon her nights, wore jeans and an old army shirt with the tails hanging out, let her hair hang loose and tangled, smoked cigarettes in a long black holder. Henry and Lorabelle talked earnestly to this wild, changed girl, now hardly recognizable as their daughter, advised caution and delay, but to no avail: she married Falbuck and went to live with him in a tiny room over a motorcycle shop. Henry and Lorabelle were left alone in the house on the hill, in peace now, with butterflies and the sound of wind in the three trees and wished she were back.

Every morning Henry took his tools and went to his work of building houses—saw the pyramid of white sand spreading out in the grass, the bricks chipping, the doors beginning to stick, the first tone of gray appearing on white lumber, the first leaf falling in the bright gutter—but kept on hammering and kept on sawing, joining boards and raising rafters; on weekends he swept the driveway and mowed the grass, in the evenings fixed the leaking faucets, tried to straighten out the disagreements with Lorabelle; and in all that he did he could see himself striving toward a condition of beauty or truth or goodness or love that did not exist, but whereas earlier in his life he had always said, "It's an illusion," and turned away, now he said, "There isn't anything else," and stayed with it; and though it cannot be said that they lived happily, exactly, and certainly not ever after, they did live. They lived—for a while—with ups and downs, good days and bad, and when it came time to die Lorabelle said, "Now we'll never be parted," and Henry smiled and kissed her and said to himself "There isn't anything else," and they died.

SEA
GIRLS

SOMETHING IS MOVING
INSIDE HIM. WHAT?
Like a hand feeling its way in darkness. He struggles up
from sleep. Perhaps a trailing dream. The vision fades as
he tries to see: the action continues but the actors have
fled, the stage is empty. He opens his eyes; the movement
ends.

Six-thirty, another half hour to sleep. Before him the
back of Hilda's head, one curl standing out on the nape,
below it some wispy black hair, the shadow of a midline
groove disappearing under her gown. He moves closer, arm
over her waist, is dozing off when he hears a whisper, low,
husky—the image of curved lips moving at his ear. He
looks at his wife, who is asleep, then realizes the sound
comes from the next room where Anneli, his daughter, is
watching television. Dawn; the shades are drawn, the room
filled with a vague gray light, like a mist; above him, at the
juncture of wall and ceiling, he can just make out the
molding, curving around the room and out of sight. In the
distance the falling note of a foghorn, unnnmm-unh: not a

warning but defeat. He thinks of ghostly ships moving in the fog and remembers something that happened thirty years ago.

He stood barefooted in smooth red pebbles, blue jeans rolled up over white legs and bony knees, looked up the beach that stretched straight away for miles in a smoking, turbulent, yet windless haze. The water was an oily greenish gray, made a hushed lapping at his feet; a few yards offshore a wall of fog boiled silently, moved slowly closer. On a dune his mother was spreading a tablecloth; his grandmother bent over a basket, exposing twitching cords behind her knees, wrinkled brown thighs. His little sister was playing in the tall grass, his father leaned against a rock reading a book. Overhead the sun was a roiled eye, shimmered and turned in a high milky overcast, glared down a thin vibrant light which picked out colors, isolated them, concentrated them as if to the point of bursting. The bald spot on his father's head glowed with bonelike whiteness, the red-checked tablecloth was in flames, the white hair falling over his grandmother's face was phosphorescent. He stared. The leaping yellow of the long curving blades of sea grass struck at his eye like swords; he turned away.

The fogbank now had reached the shore; he walked along the edge, picked up a sand dollar, ricocheted it into the murk—and heard a woman laugh, not loud, but utterly clear and very close. He peered, shocked, into the fog—had he hit someone?—listened now in an unnatural stillness, vaguely aware that a moment before there had been the sound of cars on the highway, a distant plane, foghorn, and a barking dog, but now, strangely, nothing, and the harder he listened the more impenetrable the silence became. He looked back, could see no one; the dune was out of sight. Now again the laughter, a happy silvery sound with a strangely questioning, tapering incompleteness, as if interrupted by an ambiguous gesture. It could come from no more than a few feet away. The fog boiled slowly, he moved back and forth, peering, thinking at any moment to see a boat. "Hello!" he called. Now another voice, a man's, the words distinct, yet he could not understand. At first he thought he didn't hear, but he did; then that the language was foreign, but it was not; yet he could not understand. The woman's voice again, but fainter now; they were moving away. He followed along the shore, seemed to get closer; called but could not make himself heard, shouted but could not interrupt; heard music, strings, laughter of a particular happiness and sympathy. He called louder, ran harder, and, believing himself close to the boat, ran into the water. Fog was all about him: "Wait!" he called. Water was at his waist, he could not see, raised his arms, groped forward. "Wait! Wait!" Water was at his neck, the voices became fainter. He found his way back, could hardly hear them now, ran along the shore, calling, "Wait! Wait!" fell in the sand.

Then his mother running, "Edward! What happened?" His father bending over him: "What's the matter, son?" He tried to sit up, was panting; pain in his chest and in his head, his clothes wet. He fell back on the sand, turned his face to the sea. The fog had rolled back a few feet, exposing now again a strip of slate-green water. Thin vibrant sunlight streamed down from an annunciation sky; he listened, could hear nothing but a motorcycle on the highway.

The alarm goes off; Hilda whines, kicks in simulated tantrum. He turns off the alarm, takes her in his arms, and she talks to him then in a special language of bed and sleep—in groans, moans, purrings, gruntings. He pets her, and the sounds become deeply approving: "I like that," they say; "I like that very much." He stops, and the sounds protest. She cuddles closer, twists, quivers, wanting his hand to move, to caress her; she's a small furry animal in a warm cave squirming among brothers and sisters—she delights him.

He loves her most at this time. Soon they will be at breakfast, she will be rushed, will scold as she brushes Anneli's hair, will look at her watch, think of her job— "I'm going to be late," she will say; "hurry the orange juice, I can't do everything"—a clear articulation then, reproach real not simulated, lines of strain appearing in her face. And he will remember this moment in bed, the cave of warmth, the snuggling bodies under the cover—only a half hour past, but a different world, another dimension, irrecoverable. But now in the gray light of dawn, slowly brightening, he has it, and smiles as he pets her; and she goes on in her strange happy animal talk, gradually increasing in complexity, in subtlety of inflection and meaning, until it overflows finally into human speech. She opens her eyes, laughs, kisses him on the nose, "Time to get up," she says.

He could never forget the voices in the fog, but could never remember what they had said. Many times he felt at the point of knowing, it was his own language, utterly familiar and clear, yet something would slip, and he couldn't understand. It was like a sentence the sense of which must wait in suspension pending a crucial predicate word; at any moment as he had listened that word might have precipitated meaning, but the voice had stopped, the word still missing, and the message was lost. Many times he went back to that beach, after school, riding his bicycle. He was there when fog covered both water and beach and the foghorns cried out their two-tone despair, unnnmm-unh, unnmm-unh; was there in rain and wind when the sea was hammered lead; in sparkling sunshine when it was a vertiginous blue, when he could feel the roundness of the world, the ocean clinging to it like a film of ink to a ball. But he was never there when a sheer cliff of yellowish fog came almost to the shore and the water was slate green, nor did he ever again see that kind of annunciation sky. He would stand there in all weathers, would ricochet stones and sand dollars, walk barefoot in the lace of foam, watch ships passing in the distance, until presently a friend would call, and, throwing a last stone at the elusive door, he would turn away.

He goes down to the kitchen. Anneli is lacing her shoe; Hilda is making coffee. He prepares breakfast for Whisky, the dog, goes out to the back yard to get him. Ten months old, sleek black, seventy pounds of wild playfulness, Whisky leaps, puts his head down, rolls his eyes, crouches, springs into the air, dodges, runs away, charges, growls, yelps, all with explosive exuberance like a burst of laughter. As the door is opened he streaks through, a twist of black fur, dashes through the house, claws rattling on the polished floor, slides into the kitchen. A sniff at his food but doesn't eat, must greet everyone first, nuzzles Anneli, takes her other shoe, jumps up at Hilda, surrenders the shoe after a struggle; turns to his breakfast, laps it up noisily. All happiness and sociability then, milk dripping from his mouth, he starts to nuzzle Anneli; and as Hilda tries to wipe his mouth he seizes the paper towel and runs. He bounds about the room, nudging everybody, saying hello to everybody, ducking, avoiding capture, holding the paper, tossing his head proudly high, circling under the table, between the chairs, around and around, then changing his course to a figure eight, wagging his tail, smiling, banging the table, lifting his head every few moments, sniffing, whiskers back—and it seems to Edward that the kitchen is a pool of water, shimmering, greenish, transparent water, waist-deep, and Whisky is a seal with a fish in his mouth, surfacing to snort and breathe and declare an invincible joy.

Anneli is eating a boiled egg; Hilda stands behind her brushing the black hair, Anneli twisting about to watch Whisky. "Hold still," Hilda says, pulling Anneli's head back. "Ouch!" Anneli says. Whisky circles and snorts, swims powerfully through the subtile water, nuzzles and wags his tail. Anneli turns again and a drop of egg falls on her skirt. "Now look what you've done!" Hilda says, removes the egg with a knife, "and I've no time to go cleaning you up!"; looks angrily at her watch, pulls too hard on the hair; Anneli begins to cry. "Oh I can't get anything done in here! Hold still. Edward, take out the dog, can't you?"

Hilda leaves for her job, takes the car. Edward straightens the kitchen, walks Anneli to her school, catches a bus to the city.

On the bus he sits by the window, looks out; houses pass, children with school bags. Presently a girl in a yellow dress sits beside him, the skin of her knees becoming white under the pressure of nylon stockings. Pretty knees. He looks further: legs quite shapely, the impression of a slender waist, small breasts; can't be sure. Pretending interest in a passing sports car, he looks back and sees her face. Yes, a pretty girl, very red lips and long black hair. She takes a transistor radio from her handbag; he turns toward her, hoping. "Do you *mind?*" she says haughtily. "No, no, not at all!," he says. She turns on the radio, and he hears a snatch of waltz before she changes to a newscast.

Over the years he had listened to countless radio programs, hoping to hear again the music he had heard from the fog. Sometimes, in *Nights in the Gardens of Spain* or *Der Rosenkavalier*, it would seem about to start. At any moment, he would think, there would begin that singing upward movement in the violins, becoming faster, lighter, gayer, to a pinnacle of exhilaration, then, falling like water

41

in a fountain, the melody he waited for; and if ever he
should hear it, fully, he thought, he would never lose it.
Many times it was at the tip of his tongue, in another moment he would have it. Many times he heard music that
was close, would listen, compare—is that it?—no, not quite!
The trouble, he gradually realized, was that he had heard,
not the melody itself, but an introductory passage—a passage that had disclosed intimations, one after another, of
the melody to follow, creating cumulatively a portrait of
unusual happiness, arriving at last at a point of utmost ex-
pectation, of such pressure of nascent melody that the ex-
plosion could be delayed no longer, must at the very next
moment cascade downward in an ecstasy of song—and at
just that moment it had faded.

In all the years since, he had heard it only once—or
thought he did, for he could never be certain. It was four
in the morning, and he was lost in the deserted wastes of
the Bronx, had been playing poker with friends and had
left, a loser, before the game was over; was looking for a
bus or taxi or telephone and could find none of these,
nothing; wandered along empty streets, past miles of iden-
tical apartment houses, from corner to corner, streetlight
to streetlight, examining the street signs, thinking surely
he must come soon to one he knew. A car approached from
behind; he stopped, turned, started to call, but something
strange made him pause, silent. It was a black convertible
with the top down, moving very slowly. A man was driving, a woman sat far over to the right, turned away from
the driver. The man looked straight ahead, the woman

leaned out of the car, head down, black hair falling over her left eye. A tapering white hand drooped over the car door. She wore a black dress, was beautiful but sad. They've had a fight, Edward thought. The man leaned forward, his hand to the dashboard as if to turn on the radio. The car passed slowly, the woman glancing at Edward for a moment. It was perhaps a minute later that Edward heard the theme he had heard at the beach. He ran after the car, calling, but couldn't catch it. The music faded, disappeared; he didn't know whether the car had picked up speed or the radio had been turned down. He ran for many blocks, then stood panting under a streetlight trying to hold in his ears the fading arrangement of notes. He couldn't quite get it, for it was that same intimation of melody rather than the melody itself, and after a while, seeing light in the east, he knew it was hopeless.

He takes an elevator to the nineteenth floor, greets Marie the switchboard operator, picks up his mail. His own office is on the twentieth floor, and he has started up the spiral stairway when he sees what appears to be a statue—life size, female, perhaps of a saint. The face is lowered and turned aside, the robes fall away from the slim waist in gray marble. The impression is momentary, just enough to make him stumble: this is no statue, but a live woman—a woman in a gray silk dress, with a gray face, standing by the wall with the immobility of stone—perhaps a new client in need of direction. He is continuing up the stairs, expecting her to look at him or speak, when he is jarred a second time: this is no stranger, but Liz Talman, friend and colleague. How odd that she who is all grace and quickness of movement, expressiveness of face, should stand so still, appear so grave. "Hello there," he says. "Hello," she says slowly. "You gave me a start," he says; "are you all right?" She nods and with still a faraway look goes down the hall.

The best thing about his job is the window: a large window in a small office in a tall building; it opens onto all the world, and much of the time he stands there, looking out. Around and below him is the city: buildings, billboards, tanks, towers, clocks. Down the sheer cliff on the sidewalk are the people, dots without elevation, scurrying east and scurrying west; in the street the cars, rectangles without wheels, moving on invisible currents. He sees the Embarcadero, the bay, the bridges, in the distance an airport; watches ships come and go, planes arrive and depart, above all the great arching sky, and thinks that out there, somewhere, is something that concerns him, in what way he doesn't know, but something or someone to which—or to whom—he could not be indifferent; which—or who— would not be indifferent to him. Something is waiting for him—a mystery, a puzzle, and no clue—but it's out there, he thinks, not in this room. He stands, waits, is confused. Where in all this variety should he look? Is it on that freighter now leaving the harbor empty, red Plimsoll line riding high over the water? He takes from his desk a telescope, sees a sailor leaning on the rail. Is it on that Greyhound bus now winding up the ramp to the bridge? He feels baffled, sentenced for a crime unknown to him to search always for something undefinable, unattainable because he will never know what it is. He turns from the window to his desk, and his field of vision crashes down to narrow focus. His work is to read and brief state legislation which may have bearing on insurance contracts, and he knows that, whatever it is, it's not to be found in this small print. From the hallway he hears a laugh, listens: that's Marie going to the ladies' room.

Always he had listened for the laughter from the sea. On a bus, at a movie, in a grocery store, walking on the street, wherever and whenever he saw a pretty girl he would wonder about her laugh, would glance at her legs and breasts, face and hair, thinking helplessly—sometimes smiling to himself at the ridiculousness of his thought —"Pardon me, miss, would you mind laughing for me?" But if there were anything hard, suspicious, or selfish in her face or manner he would not wonder; for the laughter he had heard and wanted to hear again was of such clarity and generosity it could not come from a small or twisted heart. Many times he felt a start of recognition, thought "that's it!" then knew it was not. It *was* up to a point, then veered away—and he came finally to realize that the laughter he once had heard was unfinished, had not run its course, was interrupted by an unseen gesture, was like that introductory passage to the melody that never quite began. He did not know the ending, the destination, of the laugh, and for this reason perhaps didn't recognize it when once, later, he did in fact hear it again. He heard it, yet didn't know he had heard it until many years later. It was during a dinner with friends, and he was telling of an evening in Venice five years previously. In the midst of his story he became aware of constraint in his listeners, paused; "I think you've told that before," his wife said. And later, in bed, "It *was* a lovely evening, but aren't you getting a bit of a bore about it?" Perhaps so, he thought, and felt sorry for himself becoming old and repetitious. What *was* so special about that night? he wondered, and after Hilda was asleep continued to puzzle about it.

It had been one of those marvelous evenings in September, neither cool nor warm, air of such balminess as to dissolve the sense of boundaries, of skin and clothing. The Piazza San Marco was filled with strolling couples; three bands were playing; happy people in light clothes were strolling about. One couple started dancing; others followed; soon the whole square was dancing. Edward and Hilda were happy, danced a long time. The throng became gayer. An American girl got up on one of the bandstands, danced solo, presently started to strip. The crowd cheered; there was loud singing; Hilda became tired, wanted to go home. They walked through the laughing people, and out of the square. It was but a short distance along a narrow street to their hotel; while crossing over a high bridge Hilda slipped, sprained her ankle.

He had told this story many times in the five intervening years but now for the first time remembered having heard on that evening the laughter he had been waiting for. They were on the bridge, there was a lapping of black water; the arrogant prow of a gondola appeared beneath them, passed full into the beam of light from a restaurant window. A woman was leaning back, her long black hair touched the water, and she laughed—that was it!—and at that moment Hilda had pitched forward with a cry, he caught her just in time, bent over her, fearing the ankle was broken, helped her, half carried her, to the hotel.

He reads the small print, smokes; the ashtray fills; at 11:30 he looks up. He senses the immense world outside the window, feels the blinders that limit his vision to small print, thinks, I don't want to live like this, I want something more. What? Travel? Maybe they can swing a trip to Europe next year; his mother would look after Anneli. But that's not enough. Look forward to it for months, finally it comes, a few weeks and it's over. He wants something more than respite, wants something different, something to stay. He wants—and it's not a luxury, he feels, but a right—that ordinary, everyday life be the real thing. And what is the real thing? He goes to the window again. Maybe it's not out there, but inside him; not to be found but achieved, something he must do.

His gaze falls on Alcatraz. He'd like to be an architect standing in wind and salt spray before a great rock, seeing with inner vision the mighty spire he will erect. A white ship is putting out to sea. He wants to be a movie producer like Fellini, setting sail for Algiers with actors, technicians, photographers, set designers—all talking, laughing, bickering—and only he seeing, in the eye of inspiration, the marvelous unity he will fuse from warring abilities and interests. Dreams. What could he do, actually? He would like to write something like *The Little Prince,* whimsical, funny, moving, for both children and grown-ups, subtly conveying some over-all view or philosophy. Last year when he had pneumonia he made a start. Should go on with it now, but has no time. Always puts it off, he thinks, always has excuses, always will regard himself as one who might have written such a book. Either you mean it or you don't, he thinks, so why not now; will never be easier. Determination blooms within him; he will begin this very day, will simply postpone other work, will write at night, weekends.

He goes to lunch, feels fine, thousands of ideas chasing around in his mind, admires the fine legs of a girl at the counter. Back in his office he gets clean paper, takes from his file the few pages he had written, reads them over, starts making corrections, feels a slow downward movement of feeling, the first intimations of a slide; tries not to notice, maybe it will go away; whistles a bit, looks around. Pictures on his desk: Anneli sitting in the sand at China Beach; Hilda at the Empire State Building, yellow sweater, hair blowing back—that was when they stayed at the St. Moritz, and she had an infection of the foot, in bed three days. Clock, calendar, pictures on the wall; moments ticking, days passing, years. He looks out at the expanse of clear sky, a faded blue; it seems far away and silent, no planes. The faint sound of a typewriter, distant laughter. Then it's on him, he can't ignore it; the slide has become an avalanche. So, he thinks, might as well face it at the beginning, stand up to it, work on through it. This is what

it's like to make something out of nothing. Or to try—
because you can never know you'll do it till it's over. Just
accept it and keep going. He continues to read and edit
and correct, he makes notes, writes; an hour passes, and
then he turns a corner in his mind, vaguely familiar, and
comes suddenly upon such a sea of despair he can't go on.

He leans at the window, looks down. That hardness at
the bottom is what's waiting for him, always at the back of
his mind, behind every thought, every diversion, at the
end of every hope, lies there now at the end of this shaft of
air, waiting, flickering, signaling their belonging to each
other. He turns back to his desk. But he never will.
There's something about this, he thinks, as about everything else, ambiguous and incomplete. He has no tragic
dimension. If he and that hardness were going to meet he
might feel some heightened meaning, or license at least.
The sidewalk is waiting, perhaps he really belongs to it,
and yet he never will. So it's true and yet not true. The
hardness is not a destiny but a companion, always there
outside the window, a waiting presence, a column of air
extending up from the pavement to his window, un-
marked but describing a fall, as clear in his mind as the
beam of a searchlight. The preoccupation earns no poig-
nance, no intensification of time; and yet the waiting
presence, the beckoning hardness, is always there, defining
him. Who is he? The man who did not jump. "As soon as
one does not kill oneself," Camus said, "one must keep
quiet about life." And he would never write that book
either. He closes the folder.

The afternoon drags on; he has a headache, goes down the hall to get an aspirin, and for a second time this day experiences a failure of recognition. In the men's lounge the shade is drawn, the room suffused with a strange amber light. As he enters he has the feeling that someone has just been here, then sees a stranger and stops; it is a man this time, in a gray suit with a somber ascetic face. After a moment the stranger begins to float to the left—in the mirrored door of the closet which hangs open before him.

He gets the car from the employment agency where Hilda works, goes to the bank to cash a check, stands in line. The woman ahead of him is young, has dark-brown hair, a graceful neck, wears a light, cotton dress. He can see the bra, sees even that it is hooked in the last holes; large bosom, probably. He steps slightly to one side: large but sags. Now she is at the window untying a dirty canvas bag, her fingernails are dirty. "Well, here we are again," she says in a nasal voice. "Nice day, isn't it?" The teller is quite pretty, greenish eyes, wears glasses with gray plastic frames; has a good mouth, soft, full, but straight, a line of brown hair on the upper lip. She wears a tight dress of natural linen, breasts held up smartly, rather pointed, dress fitting smoothly under them and tapering down, it seems, to a delicate waist which, however, is hidden by the counter; he stands on tiptoe. The woman before him finishes, turns away, brushes his hand with her hip. He stares after her, trying to preserve the tingling in his hand. "Yes?" the teller says coolly. He gives her a check for fifty dollars; she stamps it, and as she reaches to replace the stamp in the holder her right breast touches the check, moves it slightly on the counter. His mouth is dry, he swallows. "How will you have it?" she says. "I . . . , oh, . . . five tens, please."

He takes the money, turns away, almost knocks against another woman—quite short, red hair, freckles—who has come up behind him. He starts putting the bills in his wallet, looks out over the bank. There are six, no seven, girls here, most of them young. He drops a ten-dollar bill, picks it up. No, eight: one is coming out of the vault now. Three are very pretty, all wear tight skirts. One man sits at a desk near the front, handles loans. He must be the manager, doubtless has to work late sometimes . . . show a new girl the ropes. . . .

Leaving the bank, Edward starts for his car but turns suddenly, enters a tobacco shop. In front are general magazines; then comic books with covers showing rape, shooting, stabbing; paperback books with sexy covers—a shabby room seen from the doorway over the shoulder of a towering black figure, a busty girl shrinking in a corner, blouse and skirt in tatters. In the back of the shop is a counter, cigarettes, gum, cigars; behind it a thin man of about sixty with dry, grayish face, white hair. The man chats desultorily with a portly customer who leans on the counter. A small radio reports a ball game; the volume is low, they're not really listening. Edward turns left, past the paperbacks, to the more secluded part of the shop, and there on racks from floor to ceiling are the girls. The titles speak to interests in photography, sociology, art, and the dance, but nobody is fooled: these are girlie magazines and they speak to lust. He picks one off the rack, opens it at random, and there they are: scanty clothes, no clothes, the entrancing postures. He flips briskly through the pages. The two men chat idly, as if indifferent to his presence, unaware of his interest; but he feels them to be acutely aware; they know exactly what he's looking at and why; their eyes bore holes in his back; and so we are driven, driven, driven, he thinks, till we die. He flips the pages: a slender blond girl, naked, on hands and knees in the hay; his heart pounds, a sense of deafening noise in his head, yet utter silence, like the moment of ringing stunned quiet that follows a pistol shot. His hands tremble; he feels tremendous haste and guilt, as if he had wandered into the vault of a bank by mistake and were picking up bundles of thousand-dollar bills: he intends no theft but knows that, come upon, he would be viewed with dire suspicion. He leaves the shop without buying, walks quickly, then makes himself walk slowly, looks about, wonders if he has been seen.

In his car he thinks of the blond, then of the man who took the pictures. That's what I would like to be, he thinks. The photographer doesn't have much money, drives an old car, telephones the girl: "We'll do a series in the country; haystacks, gingham aprons, that kind of thing. Pick you up about nine." Comes in, finds her dressed, ready; lays hands on her, feels bra, pulls strap, lets it snap back. "What's this?" he says; "didn't I tell you last time? Leaves a red mark . . . for hours. Take it off." Runs his hands lower, feels panties. "These too. You ought to know better. Gotta be ready to work." "Okay," she says, and goes in the other room. He follows, ignoring the token wish for privacy, watches her undress. "Are you shaved?" he says. She nods. "Last time there was a black shadow," he says. "Took hours to clean up those negatives. Let me see." He examines her armpits, pubis. "No good. Let me do it." He shaves her, tickles her, and they have wild, bouncing intercourse; drive to the country, find a farm, get permission to use field and barn; he poses her stepping in and out of clothes by haystacks, in fields of clover, in stable and loft; intercourse again; drive back to town; she wants him to stay; he has other game in mind; "Be seeing you around!" he says.

A woman and child have entered the crosswalk. He's already into the intersection, going too fast. Could stop perhaps, but would slide. Goes on. The woman, holding child's hand, is in the middle of the street, flinches, glowers: "Thank *you*, Mister!" she calls as he passes. "Thank you *very much!*" She's right, he thinks, and he wants to stop, apologize; but the car behind is honking, and he goes on, thinking of Anneli and Hilda, of how angry he would be at a driver who treated them this way. And what about that blond in the hay? he thinks. He has no love to give to such a girl, no devotion, loyalty, not even interest, nothing; wants her to give to him. Transient lust on his part, adoration on hers.

He stops at a bar, orders a martini, then another; begins talking to a frowsy plump woman about forty with bleary eyes, short sandy hair that stands out from her head, good figure. For many years, she tells him, she and her husband owned a small cleaning shop; one day her husband sold it without asking her. She had worked there with him for fifteen years, helped build it up, their children worked there after school; nothing great, but security, steady customers, a good living. And he sold it. Thought he could find something better, more status, make her proud of him. Now he's out of work, can't find a job; they're living on their savings, can't send the boy to college. "It was crazy," she says; "just crazy. That's the only word for it. He was out of his mind." She thinks he ought to find another cleaning business, and he's willing now, has been looking, but can't find one he can afford. She tells Edward about steam presses, insurance, cleaning fluids, leases, the big capital outlay. "We just can't afford it," she says, "don't have that kind of money." Edward buys her a drink, wishes her luck.

Hilda and Anneli are in the kitchen. Hilda frowns as he enters, pulls away as he kisses her. "Everything's cold! I work hard all day, come home, fix your dinner, and what are you doing? Out boozing around. I won't stand for it. I just won't take it!" Whisky crouches under a chair, startled by the sudden vehemence. Anneli is drawing a horse, smiles shyly as he leans over to kiss her. "I have an earache," she says. Hilda serves dinner, begins to calm down; she's worried about Anneli, has called the pediatrician. After dinner Edward takes Anneli's temperature: 100.5°. The pediatrician comes: an infection, prescribes erythromycin, will have to be home a few days. "Who will I get to stay with her?" Hilda says; "I can't miss work again." She makes three telephone calls, finds a woman to come the next day.

In bed finally, lights out, Hilda is unhappy, tearful. "This is no way to live," she says; "I'm so rushed. This morning I was impatient, rough with Anneli. Felt bad about it all day, couldn't concentrate. I hurry to buy food, come home, cook; Anneli's sick; you're out late drinking I don't know who with and, . . . this is no way to live. I just hate it. I want to have some fun in life." "Things will get better," Edward says; "maybe we can go away." "That's what you always say," Hilda says; "it's not enough. I want something more. I want to be happy." "What's the matter, baby?" "I don't know," Hilda says; "nothing. Everything. We have a good, working relationship, and I mean *working*, could go on like this for years, till we drop —get up, go to work, do the job, then home, stove, house-work, bed, sleep—but something's missing. You don't talk to me any more, don't really look at me, seem to be listen-ing for something else." He pets her, strokes her hair, shoulders, back.

He lies awake after she is asleep, and when at last he too sleeps something soon disturbs him. Something moving. What is it? He wakes, opens his eyes. The room is dark, outside a sound of wind in trees, the cry of distant fog horns—unnnmm-unh. Hilda is snuggled against him, her breathing deep. Whisky sighs from the hallway rug. Ed-ward closes his eyes, is at the threshold of a deep sleep when he feels it again: a slow movement—unhurried, unhurriable. A door. That's it. The door in which he saw his reflection that afternoon as a stranger. Somewhere inside him a door is swinging open, the noiseless movement coming now to an end; the door is open; there's nothing there.

THE
LEAGUE
OF
DEATH

GOOD MORNING, DOCTOR.

WHAT A CHARMING OFFICE.

Beautiful rugs. That's an antique Derbend, isn't it? Magnificent. . . . A hobby of mine. That saffron is unique, comes only from the walled city on the Caspian. Wonderful condition, too. Glows like a stained-glass window. Such a thing makes the heart leap up, really a work of art. And what a magnificent view you have—such a sweep —from Bay Bridge to Farallons. Hope you don't mind my looking around. I mean no intrusion, but recognize a cultivated taste and, . . . well, I love such things.

Only analysts have such offices. And rightly, for our profession makes us prisoners. Has it ever occurred to you, how intolerable to be tied in a chair? Yet we are. The rope is invisible but the immobility is our actual life. So of course we decorate our cells, import the beauty and variety of far places, of great reaches of time, to console us. It's the least we can do. And these beautiful rugs and pictures— that watercolor, that's Van Gogh at Saint-Rémy, isn't it? . . . Lovely—they're part of the treatment; they say,

"Take heart! Man can make beautiful things!" And so, properly tax deductible. Of course I'm not really an analyst like you, but I've done a bit. Enough to know. Where shall I sit?

. . . Ah, my "problem." I like your way of putting it. Makes it sound definable. There's therapy in that already. Holds out hope, suggests that one may say "My problem is . . ." and find a way to finish. Not right away perhaps, but someday. And as soon as a problem is defined it's on the way to being solved. Isn't that right? So, let us begin. My problem is—it really *is* quite simple now that I think of it—my problem is boredom.

I know boredom, doctor, as do few others. Have lived with it, absorbed its quality, taste, felt its weight on my bones. Look, that wall of fog outside the Golden Gate—see the slow relentless boiling? It will sweep in after a while under the bridge, extinguish every sparkling point of light and water, every bright sail, will rise, envelop the city, the hills, may enter even this room up to the ceiling. A sinister and fatal boredom, like that fog, churns at the edges of my life, is never far away; rolls in, creeps in, worms in; into mouth and lungs, a gray gorge rising, choking me, rising higher, behind my eyes. I've grappled with it for years— only that's just the trouble, you can't grapple with fog, there's no hand-hold. On countless days I've looked out on such a scene as this—my office has the same view—on such splendor, and felt like a prisoner on Alcatraz. But they were luckier; could believe that bars confined them, dream of release or escape, while I know the prison to be the walls of my skull, or some stiffening perimeter of spirit, perhaps, and no getting away. Oh, I know boredom.

. . . Hard to say, I don't know that I'm bored *about* anything. More like the color of hair: boredom pertains to me as, say, hope to others. Look, it's not so complicated: if you're committed to people you're not bored, if you're not you are. It's that simple. We just don't like it. And being committed to people means doing something for them —teaching a class, building a house, fixing a car—not just a job, but putting some heart in it. But when you've done that for a while, whatever it is, and got good at it, just then the corruption begins. It seeps in through the first cracks— some indifference, some cutting of corners—the cracks get bigger, and then one day your heart's not in it any more. The work goes on, looks pretty much the same from the outisde, but now it's more for the money or to keep busy or distract yourself or maybe to pretend that nothing is changed. That's when you get bored. You know what I mean? Somehow the forms of social committment betray us, slip away; the visions of service become shabby. They stand around in our minds still, like the dusty scenery of some old play, but generate no action. It happens to all of us, to you too perhaps? No?

. . . Ah you're a pro and not one to tip your hand. I recognize technique. The analyst, like the Oracle at Delphi, neither conceals nor reveals, but *indicates*. No matter. Maybe you're one of the happy few. But surely you've noticed your colleagues? . . . Anyway it is in truth the story of my life which, you will be relieved to hear, I'm not going to relate. For you to place me it will suffice to know that, having dipped with successive disillusionments into several fields of service to man, I chose finally the law; and by the time that profession had been mastered and its ideal of justice irrecoverably buried in money, self-interest, red tape, and indifference, it seemed too late to make another major change; the course of my life was set, and it was then the great gray tide of boredom swept in as if never to recede.

Outwardly nothing changed, nobody noticed. I received clients, argued cases, if anything was more successful. But the drive was gone and inside all was different. I was drifting. I used to read the journals; now I couldn't stand them, found them nauseating; and one day, thumbing through an issue of the *International Law Review,* I couldn't find a single article, including one of my own, that might not just as well never have been written. I began to read fiction, came upon good novels, spoke of them enthusiastically, but never finished them; they lay about the house, bits of paper sticking out of their middles, until gathered up finally and put away on shelves. Coming to the end of books I began with things. Nothing lasts. Within the limits of destructiveness I permitted myself there was not enough distraction—in any thing, person, or pursuit.

But I have found a cure for boredom. You won't like it at first. Fasten your seat-belt; it takes some getting used to. It's the idea of death.

. . . Is our time up? . . . A few minutes more? You're a pro all right, I can tell; I, too. We never get drawn in, ring the bell at fifty minutes no matter what. Footsteps of a rapist on the stairs? Grandfather dying? Plane crashing? No matter. Time's up. How do *you* say it? . . . Never mind, I'll hear in a minute. I always say, "We must stop now"—in a gentle, reluctant tone, as if it were difficult for me, too, to interrupt. We sell time, can no more forget the clock than the greengrocer his scales.

. . . A glance at your watch, that's all. The slightest of movements. Rude of me to notice. Forgive me. In my office—this may interest you—I have a clock on a bookshelf behind my patient's head; by an almost imperceptible deflection of gaze I can see the time. But still it's perceptible. Patients always notice, they just don't say. It's such a bore to be watched—don't you agree?—and such a strain. That's the great advantage of the couch. All psychotherapies tend toward the couch, not just Freudian. It's the weariness of the therapist not the requirements of his theory that lays a patient on his back.

When do you want me again? . . . Fine. Five o'clock Tuesday.

. . . No, no, that's all right. I understand, perfectly. It's the same old out. Fascinating to hear these things from the other end. We all do it, one way or another, all of us who are lucky enough to be in demand: we select. Without openly rejecting anybody we find ways to choose patients who have money; that's first of course, and who, beyond that, are of some interest: intelligent or pleasing perhaps, or who won't be too hostile or threaten suicide or call us at home. Don't be embarrassed, you're not alone. My particular way—would you like to hear? It's worth while I think to compare notes; we learn from each other—I make my pitch at the end of the first hour, just like you. "I don't have time," I say, "to take you on in therapy just now. My schedule's full, and there are some people waiting. But I do have time to see you once or twice more in consultation, to help you evaluate the problem, decide what to do, and, if therapy is needed, see you to competent hands." This way I'm never committed to a patient until I know a good deal about him. I remain free to refer him, put him on my waiting list, or take him on immediately; for of course, if he should prove a millionarie, an "unexpected vacancy" can always occur. Not so different, you see, though you were more deft. If one's not in demand, of course, you have no choice; when a colleague calls with "Can you take a patient?" you simply have to swallow and say yes, thank you very much, and hope for the best.

Anyway, have no concern: I don't seek treatment. I shall impose upon your time—if you are willing—for only five hours. Five of these precisely measured fifty-minute hours. . . . Because—and this is a confession, I should have told you sooner—I'm not here on my own motivation but my wife's. Always she wanted me to come, and always I scoffed. "It wouldn't help," I'd tell her, "I know too much." She'd put her arms around my neck, twist her fingers in my hair; "Just for a consultation," she would say; "talk things over. An evaluation. Five hours." "Hoping I'll pick up enough transference to make me stick?" I would say. She'd hide her face on my shoulder, tears wetting my shirt, press against me, plead, "For me, for me. . . ." She was getting weak, knew she couldn't help me, and I never did . . . while she lived. I come now for her, a gesture, like lighting a candle. For of all persons I have known, not excepting myself, she's the only one I respect.

So—five hours with an analyst in honor of my wife!

. . . Ah yes. "Time now." How clean. I like that. Tuesday at five. *Au revoir.*

II

Good afternoon, doctor. You look tired. Tuesday is perhaps a bad day? It is for me: the pleasures of the weekend already forgotten in the strain of Monday; the weekend to come still too far away to lift one's spirit. And five o'clock is the nadir of this low day. You've seen nine patients, I imagine, and two to go. You have a right to be tired. I work the same way, and never at a loss for a creditable reason, but suspect all reasons. You know what my accountant said? "You're a money-making machine. IBM should copy you."

. . . This chatter bothers you, I think. You want me to get down to business. . . . Ah, my cure for boredom. I'm glad you ask. It's my major interest, my life work, there's nothing I'd rather tell you.

It goes back a long time; I discovered the cure, in fact, before I knew the ailment. Death was the whole of my childhood: the broken doll, the stuffing coming out of my teddy bear, the flies and mosquitoes killed without a thought, the snail stepped on after a rain. Everywhere I looked there it was, and sometimes terribly close: once my mother dropping a live lobster into boiling water, and I simply could not believe that this was she who tucked me in and drove away my demons at night. How can one reconcile such images? If you're interested in psychodynamics, doctor, put that down as the primal scene for me, the trauma that shaped the future. It was then, I think, that death got in my eyes, and ever since they've been still and make people uneasy. In the car by my father I would watch with dread for the next smear of fur and gore; and after a while I wouldn't get in a car. I refused to eat meat, became thin. One day as I got up from the table my father said, "That belt you're wearing, 'Genuine Cowhide'." "I'll use a string," I said. "And your shoes," he went on, "you know what they are?" "I'll go barefooted." "And the sweatband of your cap?" I threw it in the corner. He took my ball, tossed it lightly; he was relentless: "Now this," he said, "is covered with the skin of a horse." So I was defeated, knew that my hands too were red, went back to eating meat and never felt innocent again.

I was fascinated with the situation of the condemned, would go to the movies and sit biting my fingernails. There would be Greta Garbo in prison talking to her blind lover, knowing she would face a firing squad at dawn; a lieutenant sitting at a table in a dugout, candle sputtering, artillery fire outside, dirt falling between the overhead timbers, writing to his wife before a mission from which he would not return; a murderer on death row, the last night, the visit of the priest, the key in the lock. I would come out of the theater into the bright light, blinking, would put myself in the place of the characters I had seen, try to feel what they must feel, and, in their experience, deal with my own death. Yet never did I understand the condemned, had not the empathy for such a leap; at the last moment imagination, perhaps courage too, would draw back and their condition would remain alien. I stood on my side and looked at them on theirs. It wasn't far; but eyeing the abyss between, I would feel a shudder of revulsion, as if attempting to experience something which, *if* experienced, would contradict me.

I liked to walk, but in the greenest forest found rotting logs and dying flowers. I walked then on city streets until one day there was a crash and shower of glass, and a dark-haired woman with blood on her face was screaming; and while the car smoked and people stood by saying "Call an ambulance!" I pulled her out, and she lived—her companion died—and everybody said how brave I was. But the others forgot, while the crash kept sounding in my mind, the glass splinters tinkling down, the scream echoing; and it came to me suddenly that to live under sentence of death is not a rare predicament to be known vicariously but the human condition and that the revulsion I had felt, as at something alien, was but a shudder of recognition. I had looked across no chasm but into a mirror. The woman's blood stayed red for me, and I gave up walking, lived alone in a furnished room, drew the shades.

There was little to do there but read, and in reading I

found that death is the chief awareness of our age. "Someone must have been telling lies about Joseph K.," said Kafka, "for without having done anything wrong he was arrested one fine morning." Someone has indeed been telling lies; *we* have, for centuries; and when finally they get brushed away a sentence of death is exposed. Copernicus swept out a pretty big lie; Darwin and Einstein tossed out two more. The pace of this housekeeping gets faster all the time, and by now the cupboard is nearly bare of the great lies we call absolute verities, and that's all we ever had to hide death. After the First World War we took time out of its secret pocket and put it on our wrist and now everybody can hear the tick. I heard it very loud. I sat there alone and read, and after a while began to feel myself dying.

It was there that Mariette found me. She was the landlord's daughter, and one evening—the fourth of July, as I learned—she came in my room, raised the shades, and said, "Look at the beautiful bursts of light, yellow and green and blue and red. Look at the fountain of fire!" She came back often, looked in my eyes and was unafraid. She didn't like to be indoors, wanted sun and wind on her skin, made me walk with her. She laughed, looked everywhere and always saw something beautiful. We fell in love, were married.

"What shall I do?" I said, looked in her face, and found no answer. I became a partner in a trucking firm, bought a fine house, drove a Lincoln; was bored. "It's an accumulation of *things*," I said. "I want life to *mean* something."

"Better it *be* something," Mariette said. "I don't want to live just for myself," I said. "Look at the swallows building a nest," she said. I studied economics, mastered price theory, became an advisor to the Department of Commerce; and was bored. "Why does everything fail?" I said. "Look at the yellow leaves," Mariette said. "I don't want to look at any god-damned leaves!" I shouted. "I'm looking for meaning, don't know where I'll find it, but not up any tree." I studied philosophy, learned about essence, appearance, reality; and was bored. "Why can't I make anything last?" I said. "Look at the storm clouds," Mariette said. I changed to law, studied due process, equal rights, argued with brilliance, wrote books, became rich; and was bored. It was the same in law as everywhere else and too late then for still another change, and the great gray tide swept in, over me, as if to stay.

I turned back then to death. Only the bored have the leisure, the reflectiveness, and above all the proper frame of mind to study death. Because—do you know?—everything we do to fight boredom has a death-tasting quality. Have you noticed? Gambling, adultery, LSD—that sort of thing. Anything healthy is useless. So—our life is under the ax with an indeterminate but limited stay of execution. What does it mean? What can one make of it? Not much, I thought—we die, that's it. And most people if they consider it at all find it gloomy, I too.

Gradually, however, my view changed. I discovered the significance of death to be precisely opposite to what I had supposed: it is not the enemy of life but life's great pillar, support. A world without death would be a world without birth, hence without change, without creation, eventually without movement, a frozen moment infinitely extended; and can you think of any good—tell me frankly, doctor—can you imagine any value, any pleasure, any lovely sensation that could survive in such a tableau? I could not. Our condition, therefore, must be regarded as fortunate; for death, which our age had discovered, in a sense, was in fact the source of meaning. We had come full circle: the collapse of value had burdened us with death, now death would create value. A fire becomes, not less, but more truly a fire as it burns faster. It's the being consumed that pushes back the darkness, illumines whatever there is of good in our days and nights. If it weren't brief it wouldn't be precious. Let me say it flatly: We are lucky we die, and anyone who pushes away the awareness of death lives but half a life. Pity him!

In the excitement of these ideas boredom vanished. On every possible occasion—cocktail party, board meeting, bridge game—I spoke of death. Not with gloom, but humor and verve. And was met—this won't surprise you, doctor, but it did me—with stunning indifference, even hostility. People would not hear me out, would interrupt, turn away, change the subject. Invitations stopped, my phone didn't ring. Now here was a curious business. I was saying nothing new: in the flat consciousness of modern man death stands out like an obelisk. How did I offend?

Well, you know the answer. We want to forget this great thing we have learned. It's a wild wind in our lives, tossing aside like scraps of old paper the illusions we live by. We want to shut it out, close the doors and windows and go back to the old rocking chair, the old dozing before the fire, the old conforting myths of some special appointment in this otherwise indifferent universe. Hence the paradox: We retain the liveliest admiration for the artists and philosophers who have set forth our awareness of death, crown them with laurel, but forget their message.

It was, however, this public apathy that inspired me with the single most important idea of my life, the League of Death. Only a few free spirits at the leading edge of the modern consciousness are truly aware of death; the rest have chosen to ignore or forget. But this awareness is too valuable to remain with the few. Our times have suffered the ruin of traditional values, we are adrift in a sea of nihilism, lost, and not trying to find the way back because we don't believe there *is* a way to find, or a place to go, or even a star to steer by. Nothing matters, says the modern mood, so why be our brother's keeper? why create? why care? Yet there *is* a way and we have the clue, lack only the nerve to use it. Death is the way—not the way back but the way *on*—to greater good, to conscience, to social commitment, to that ever-elusive brotherhood of man. This great insight, I resolved, would not remain with the few. I would ignite the idea of death in the mind of every man, woman, and child in the country—perhaps, as I began to think, in the whole world.

I decided to found an organization which would bring to this project the techniques of Madison Avenue. The idea must gain access to mass communication, enlist the entertainment industry, be cast in forms accessible to every level of intellect and sophistication. I began to invent ditties of death for radio, skits for television, discovered in myself a strange brilliance, inventiveness; a great profusion of ideas tumbled about in my brain. I could see a huge billboard of a heart with a coronary occlusion, and the caption: "How may more ticks in *your* old ticker?" Or a single cancer cell saying, "You'll never know I'm with you till I've got a million friends. Live today!" Or the Grim Reaper urging caution on the road, strict observance of speed limits, saying, "Drive safely, friend, . . . I'll meet you at home!" The flavor of death enhances the flavor of everything else, so I would sell it to advertisers. For Troy Beer, a delicate skull on the can, with the slogan, "The face that launched a thousand ships. Drink up!" I would persuade orchestras to begin each program with a funeral march: to even the gayest waltz a bit of dirge adds zest. I dreamt of a vast international organization with headquarters like the Time-Life Building, began to have fantasies of greatness, even—I confess it—the Nobel Prize.

But not for long. With the start of my campaign hostile rebuff became my daily bread. No foundation would give me money. I had raised large sums for political parties, for museums, guide dogs; but now, with a truly great cause, I couldn't raise a dime. NIMH was not interested; the Department of Health, Education and Welfare wouldn't hear me out; on Madison Avenue I couldn't get past the secretaries. When I surrendered my pride and wrote to friends, nothing but silence. From office to office I trudged with my great idea, my bulging portfolio of posters and jingles and slogans, but doors do not swing open to death. I felt I was crying out behind thick glass; people glanced briefly, seemed irked by my urgent gesticulations, and passed on, having heard nothing.

It was the same old story: death is a blinding glare, and people won't look. Oh, they know about it, and the voice of genius may occasionally charm them into taking a peek, but not much more than a peek. They were not, at any rate, to be persuaded by the likes of me to accept it as proper illumination for their everyday lives; it gave too much light, exposed too much as sham. "Take it away," they seemed to say; "and since you're haunted by it, away with you too!" I walked the streets, knocked on doors, preached on street corners and in parks; the soles of my shoes wore thin, my clothes were shabby; and wherever I went people cast on me a cold eye. "Don't tell us about death," they seemed to say; "just *die!*"

Then one day, quite suddenly, I gave up. To hell with it; they don't want my help, won't hear me, spit in my face. Let them be damned. There's much fun to be had and not much life to have it in, and too much of it wasted already, preaching to deaf men in a stone wilderness. I went back to the practice of law, back to my teak office and my gray flannel suit; and, to my surprise, was welcomed by colleagues. They seemed a little guilty at having rejected me as prophet, and I exploited this with a trace of wistfulness in an otherwise flawless urbanity. I went back to the corporation tax cases for which I had a flair, back to the money and the gambling, back, in short, to being a pillar of society. The fun, however, was short lived; for I had returned, also, as it transpired, to boredom.

. . . Good stopping place, doctor. You couldn't have hit it better. . . . Friday at three? Okay.

III

Good afternoon, doctor. And how are you? . . . I've not much heart for it today. Except for Mariette I'd have canceled. I'll carry on though. The memorial service in which you are so kindly participating is half over.

Occasionally during the months following my return to the law I would get strange muttering telephone calls from people who wanted to talk about death. Some of the seed I had sown had taken root apparently, but in meager cracks and crevices; for the characters who began to appear at my elegant chambers were of strange twisted shapes. Bearded men, smelly men, men with twitches, with dirty fingernails, men without ties or jackets, one without shoes. They ruffled a smooth office routine, jarred my rich clients, scratched and belched and picked their noses in the waiting room; and one and all they gave my secretary the willies. I would see them and they would talk; I would watch and listen and send them away after a while; and in a few days they would be back. They came ostensibly to learn about death; but I didn't believe it. My theory was simple: I could explain it, as you have seen, in a few minutes. These people kept coming, talked more and more about themselves, their problems, life-stories, less and less about death.

. . . Ah, I see you have grasped already what took me some months to realize: I had become a psychotherapist. Not surprising, I suppose; our field attracts strange talents. What did surprise me, though, was how good I was. These people were borderline at best, many of them outright psychotic; yet in the course of a few months they were well. Not just improved, really well. Ah, you smile. . . . I know; what is "really well"? I mean, specifically, that these bitter, deviant, ill-fed, often delusional clients of mine—patients, as I began to call them—became productive, useful, happy, capable of love. And what else can "well" mean? And can you guess what they did with their newfound mental health? They became therapists, began treating others as I had treated them. Before long my work was divided between a lucrative but meaningless practice of law, and a psychiatric practice which brought no income but was of vital importance.

Only after some months did I realize the full import of what had happened. My League of Death had failed to launch the mass movement I had wanted, but had achieved an elite I had not thought to hope for. The creative process is an invincible mystery: we labor, strive to give birth, we strain, bear down, break our hearts, and only as we despair notice something unintended, more valuable than the end we had in view. These are moments of cosmic justice: the by-product worth more than the product for which the factory was built; the solvent meant for discard containing the miracle drug. I had worked for a philosphic revolution and, in failing, had created a powerful weapon against the nihilism of our times. I called it thanatotherapy.

My boredom was lost in a great surge of enthusiasm. Again I left the practice of law, gave over my whole time to the creation of an organization. In our field every new discovery has to be institutionalized—as you, doctor, must know very well. Can't survive otherwise. Anyway, I and three of my former patients, now colleagues, formed the A.T.A., American Thanatotherapy Association. We adopted a constitution, elected officers (I was president, of course), founded a journal, and applied for a charter.

And the moment we had an identity the slander began. We were called crackpots, deathpots, pallbearers, life-haters, spooks; were hated by medicine, psychiatry, the academicians, and most of all by psychoanalysts. Even the government joined the attack: Internal Revenue ruled that we were not an educational organization, but a club—imagine the insult!—that dues were nondeductible. Universities closed their doors to us, the state refused us a charter, the press lampooned us.

Yet all this was fortunate in a way; it put us on our mettle, forced us to tighten our belts, impose upon ourselves rigorous standards. We established an Institute of Thanatotherapy, offered training-thanatotherapies for students, thanato-research methodology, advanced courses in thanatechnics, and metathanatology. We made it our policy never to graduate anyone; for the education of a true therapist—as I need hardly tell you, doctor; everyone knows your continuing study of the late anal stage—must go on forever. Only posthumously would we grant a diploma. The danger besetting us was the common one to which people everywhere succumb, that we would turn away from death, allow the vision to fade. To combat this tendency I would close each meeting with an inspirational film: cancer, syphilis, executions, war films—that sort of thing. I ruled my little group with an iron hand, always as a matter of policy harder on myself than anyone else. When our seminars broke up, usually about midnight, I would begin my solitary work: clinical notes and observations, progress reports on students, papers for our journal. I was seldom in bed before three, up again at seven to patients, students, colleagues, committees.

The rest, as you know, is history. The AMA filed an injunction, we fought and lost, appealed and lost, carried it finally to the Supreme Court, and won. The lucky break was my being called in when the governor went berserk. I knew him well from my days in law, found him now at the door of his room high up in the Mark Hopkins, stark naked, pointing a gun at me, saying he would shoot me dead if I took another step. "Gun," "shoot," "dead"—what were these to me? Old friends, basic concepts you might say. I simply took the gun, pushed him into his room, closed the door, and gave him an intensive session of thanatotherapy; when we came out together four hours later to the glare of flashbulbs and television the governor was his normal political self: dark blue suit, cheery hello for the reporters, a smile and a wave for the cameras, the promise of a complete explanation, and a hint that the whole thing was a communist plot. Well, that put us on the map; the psychoanalysts scoffed—nothing appeases an analyst—but the State Director of Mental Hygiene sat up and took notice. Gradually the persecution lost force; our therapeutic successes were becoming better known; we cured cases with which your group, doctor—I mean no respect—failed utterly. . . . Oh, I meant "disrespect." So, you've found me out, but let us not tarry on trifles.

More and more people came for treatment, not just deviants now but solid citizens. We raised our fees; the beatniks could no longer afford us; our field had become the great middle class, a bottomless reservoir of maladjustment, as you know. More and more students applied for training; we raised our fees again; we had been struck by success. We wouldn't recognize it at first, were too attached to our role of outcast, but when I was asked to address the social workers it could no longer be denied: we were in.

My colleagues were happy, but I was worried; and as it turned out, I had reason. What seemed the beginning of a golden age for thanatotherapy was the beginning, rather, of the end. Success is a burden and a threat; I tried to be equal to it, to guard my group against it, but failed. We were getting bored with death. I observed chatting and passing of notes during a lecture on hemorrhage, and one evening saw my most gifted disciple yawn during a concentration camp film. Youth, health, high spirits had always endangered our basic concept; now money and social acceptance had been added, and proved too much. The idea of death was fading; the illusion of immortality was sneaking back, wrapping us in cotton batting, and as our work became more successful it became meaningless. Our patients still improved—what that means I can't imagine, unless perhaps they get better no matter what—but we who were doing the therapy, we were dying without knowing it. I knew it, cried an alarm, but was not heard.

But I mislead you, make it seem that I was steadfast as others faltered. In fact I moved with the current, with more awareness perhaps but just as fast, and one day looking in the mirror I took inventory and found the transformation complete. I saw a man of distinguished appearance, gray hair, dignity of bearing, composure, elegant grooming; dark suit of Italian silk, Sea Island shirt, Swiss tie, gold watch. He stood in a room like this one, nineteen stories up in a tower of steel and glass, with great windows from floor to ceiling giving upon this incomparable view; teak furniture, Turkoman rugs, lapis ashtrays, concealed bar, stereophonic high-fi, an Aston-Martin in the garage—and how much longer to live? to what purpose? He didn't care. He made as much money, this man I observed, as ever he had at law, and, I realized suddenly, was just as bored. How had all this happened? Where was death? Where my great insight, comforter, inspiration? Where the dark and glorious companion of desperate battles?

I didn't know, couldn't find him, wouldn't try. Death

was something vaguely unpleasant, unreal, far off; neither inspired nor terrified; happened to other people. It happened to soldiers in Vietnam, to Jews in Auschwitz, to civil-rights workers in Dixie, to passengers in unlucky airplanes: happened most of all to people in newspapers and was not very important.

My creative work had ended. In the evenings I drank martinis, wine with dinner, read the paper, fell asleep. My practice flourished. From the nooks and crannies of this city—the plushiest of nooks, most elegant of crannies—my patients came, tracing out invisible paths to my door, ringing my bell, entering, to speak to me. Ten a day, waiting list, high fees. It wasn't hard. I had given up teaching them about death; they wouldn't listen, didn't want to know, wanted only to talk; and I had long since learned to put them on the couch, it's much easier that way. My work, you see, had lost its distinguishing marks, was not really thanatotherapy but pretty much anybody's therapy. They came and talked and talked and talked, and I listened. Or rather I listened when I could; much of the time I was bored, my thoughts would drift on their own currents. My reputation was never better, some people thought me a genius, but *I* knew my heart was no longer in it. I wasn't trying. You are an honorable man, doctor, and it shames me to admit this, but there's no point coming to an analyst and hiding things: my work was shot through with a fraudulence so subtle no one suspected, no one could have proved, but I knew. I was a highwayman of the age of anxiety. No weapon, never left my room, but a highwayman nonetheless—of such guile that my victims would line up at my door, waiting for the privilege of surrendering their secrets and their money. And what was the nature of my art? I charmed them by embodying their illusions, so offering a tangible basis for their hopes. I divested them of their money, leaving their illusions—with which they would not have parted anyway—and protected them from what I knew: that what they sought is not to be found, that nothing else is certain but that we come to a bad end.

. . . I'm ready. Same time next week? . . . I'll be here.

IV

Good afternoon, doctor. And have you been waiting eagerly all week for the continuation of my tale? That's a nasty crack. Forgive me. I want to have done with it. I'll plunge right in.

One day during a therapy session a remarkable thing happened. My patient was a young stockbroker whom I had been seeing three times a week for about a year. He had a soft face, a deferent furtive smile, and would hardly raise his eyes as he entered my office; would lie on the couch before I had finished closing the door, spread his legs, feet falling outward, and would start talking before I was seated. I see from your expression you know the type. He had recently been married and spent most of the time complaining about his wife: "I just . . . don't under-stand. . . ." "I just . . . can't see why she . . ." "I just . . ." His speech was mumbling and indirect; and, in the plaintive note he imparted to that word "just"—as if he asked so little of life it were inexcusable he should not get it—he gave voice to fear and weakness. I don't remember what he was talking about during the hour in question. To be frank I had not for some weeks been paying much attention and in retrospect can infer a paranoid break which I had not noticed. I was bored and, on that particular day, also sleepy. My mind floated away: the fine legs of the young woman who had just left . . . must get a haircut tomorrow . . . order a case of *Château Laffitte-Rothschild* '59. Then a blank, I must have dozed off. The next thing I knew my patient was sitting in the chair in front of me, a revolver in his hand, saying, "And now, doctor, I'm going to kill you." I did not panic but came wide awake and gave him my full attention. "What will you say," I asked, "when the police question you?" He didn't answer. "You'll have to tell them something," I went on reasonably, "will have to explain yourself. We might as well work it out now. I'll help you. I am, indeed, well placed to do this; for not only am I trained in these matters and know you very well but also am the victim of the act to be investigated. Tell me, how *do* you understand your motives?" I kept on in this seductively reasonable way and got him talking finally, and so the strange hour proceeded; he kept the gun on me, with some occasional cockings and uncockings to tease me. "We must stop now," I said when his hour was up. He made no move. After a few moments I took a chance: pressed the button for my next patient and stood up, saying, "See you Tuesday, usual time." He hesitated a moment, put away the gun, and left.

Alone, I found myself drenched in sweat, my hands trembling. I canceled my next two appointments, had a martini, and went for a walk by the sea. My intention was to call the police, have him picked up and committed, but kept putting it off and finally did nothing. He had scared hell out of me but also interested me, and I wanted to see him again. It was the second time I had conducted psychotherapy at gunpoint; I was becoming a specialist.

As the time came on Tuesday I was quaking with regret, mouth dry, knees trembling, but too late now to change my mind. I rang the buzzer, and there he was. He ignored my outstretched hand, ignored the couch, went straight to the chair, and drew his revolver. "So, what's new?" I said, and thus began our session. It went on like this for three weeks—nine sessions with that gun aimed at me. A most extraordinary case, I really ought to publish it. Do you realize, doctor, when you face a loaded revolver, though you can't see the bullet in the chamber, you can see the lead noses of the others gleaming dully in their dark nests? Creates quite a feeling of authenticity.

Does this interest you, doctor? . . . Yes? Good. It did me, enormously. And there are two things I can tell you about my work with this patient. First, I was not bored. Not in the slightest, and not sleepy either. Second, I was an exquisitely attuned therapeutic intelligence. Always I had been a good therapist—when I paid attention—but this time, pardon my bluntness, I was superb: sensitive, intuitive, empathic, sparing of interventions, warm in manner yet detached, interpretations pithy, timely, sometimes even witty. Your old Sigmund himself would have been impressed, believe me. And in just three weeks a far-reaching system of paranoid delusions had been worked through. He put away the gun, we continued vis-à-vis for five more sessions, then terminated by mutual agreement, the treatment a complete success. That was six months ago; I hear from him occasionally. No relapses so far; he's getting along fine.

In retrospect what struck me most forcibly was my vitality, the sense of purpose and meaning. The problem was how to hold on to this, how extend it. It was death, of course—just closer than usual. . . . Closer. . . . But that's *it!* I realized suddenly, that's the secret. Thus I came upon my second most revolutionary discovery: death must be courted. Recognition is not enough; pursuit is mandatory.

My first applications of this insight failed; I was trying, as I see in retrospect, to duplicate in a simply mechanical way the conditions under which I had recovered meaning. I concealed in a shoebox on my bookshelf a loaded and cocked revolver, so mounted as to point at my heart as I sat behind the couch. It didn't work: folklore to the contrary notwithstanding, guns don't go off by themselves; I knew there was no danger, and soon I was bored. Next I put a live white mouse in the box, and it was then that Mariette left me. She had a literal mind and simply could not understand my researches. She argued with me, said I was crazy, begged me to see a psychiatrist; she shouted, threatened, beat her fists on me, wept. "I have to leave you my poor crazy darling," she said finally, "or you'll kill me too." And she left. Anyway, the mouse didn't work either. It created danger all right, but I listened only for the mouse, paid no attention to my patients. It was hazard without meaning, unrelated to what I was doing. These two failures, however, led to the crucial modification of my theory, the crowning touch as I now see it: The risk of death must be intrinsic to the pursuit of value. Whatever you find in life of meaning or desire you must strive for so hard, with such recklessness and courage, as to increase the likelihood of death.

Now here was an insight to redeem our group. The younger members, I realized, might not buy it—I felt separated from them by some gulf of age and despair—but my senior colleagues, the three with whom I had founded the organization, they might understand, and the four of us together could swing the rest.

I summoned them and prepared myself for a crucial encounter, the severest test of logic and persuasion. When the time came I rose and stood before them, silent, watching. The room was heavy with smoke, dimly lighted by a flickering red candle, windows and doors hung with black crepe. A hush fell as they felt the impact of my waiting. I immobilized them in the heaviness of my gaze, crushed back their vision, made them look inside their skulls, hear their heartbeats, feel the paltry span, each beat diminishing by one the few remaining. When finally I spoke it was, I believe I can say this, with compelling conviction and eloquence.

"We pretend, gentlemen, to be aware of the ax. But I must tell you we forget, we lie, live basely with the illusion of continuing life." I presented, then, my new theory, captured them with its irrefutable logic, came to my peroration. "Stay with the Main Show, my friends. Never be drawn into side issues, entertainments. Stay right there at the center ring in the big top. And what is the Main Show? Ah, . . . you know, have only to listen to the muffled drum within, . . . you *know!* How to live, . . . the despair, . . . the great cutting edge on which your life is turning—that is the Main Show. Never leave it. A man is up there in the big top, the highest point, right under the canvas—see him!—there! hanging by his teeth, arms outstretched, spinning and turning. The colored spotlights play over him, the drums begin to roll. Most people are watching the dancing bears, but you, my friends, must fix your gaze on the dangling man. He's going to fall in a minute, any moment now, and there's nothing to be done about that, there's no net; but in the meantime he may achieve something truly remarkable, some glittering stunt perhaps, even a moment of heartbreaking beauty. *The man is you:* Stay with him. Don't run away from yourself. It is not important that you be happy or that you be sad, that you live long or that you live short; what is important is that you live authentically. Do not run from the true condition of your life. Hold still, feel the cutting edge on your throat, watch the dangling man, study his condition. What in this precarious and fateful state can he still do?

That, when you find it, is your task, your true vocation!"

There was not a dry eye in the room, and this reassured me, at a time when belief in myself was ebbing, that I did have a message, and that—though the world is fiercely armored against it—to some it would get through. This cheers me on, even now.

When they asked how, specifically, to apply this insight I gave them a simple formula: "Imagine you have a fatal disease and one week to live. How would you live differently? Apply then the mandate of that limited life to your life now." They understood, and I called upon them, one by one, to stand and declare themselves. Jimmy, puffing on his pipe, getting gray, a short thoughtful man with a sad, lined face, spent all his money on sports cars, lived in San Rafael, drove an XKE: "I'd come down the Waldo Grade at a hundred and fifty miles an hour." Charlie, who had been exploited, insulted, persecuted for years by a sadistic brother-in-law: "I'd kill the son of a bitch!" Dr. Heppleman, sixty-seven years old, had taught mathematics in a state college before becoming a thanatotherapist, wise old face crinkled with a beatific smile: "One of my patients," he began dreamily in his high, piping voice, "is a Miss Jameson, a blond, in treatment for years, a hysteric with a fear of falling. She lies on the couch, her breasts like mountains in Eden, her hips moving slightly, as she struggles for words to express sensations she does not permit herself to feel. Well, . . . if I had just a week I think I would tell her tomorrow, 'Miss Jameson, I can no longer be your therapist. I have fallen in love with you.' "

That really broke us up—the image of that shy old man sitting behind the couch leching after his pretty patient. We simply rolled and roared with laughter, and it's a measure of Hep's gentleness and good humor that he could laugh with us, his little red eyes twinkling with lust. I walked home that evening with a great quiet exhilaration, knowing that I had brought our organization and my own life to a major turning point.

And what about me? What would I do? With dismay I found I couldn't answer, didn't know. I had never wanted anything but meaning, value, the social good—what else is there?—and I could think of no way to pursue these things with more passion or risk than I had been doing all along. Had I, then, all these years been following the prescription I had just now formulated? It would seem so. But then why had I been bored? A strangeness settled on my spirit; I was becoming a mystery to myself, felt alienated from my friends who found such quick brave answers.

For a while there was great vitality in our group. All but I began to burn, as Walter Pater had advised, with a hard gemlike flame. Not for long, but that was to be expected; bright fires are brief. The important thing was that boredom had given way to value. There was unusual warmth and comradeliness among us; we had that independence of possessions, that freedom and generosity of soldiers before a battle. My friends were proud of what they were doing, wanted to share it with me; and I was proud for them.

It meant a great deal to Jimmy that I would get up at

five in the morning to watch him drive. And what an experience to stand there at Vista Point in the gray dawn when the first trace of pink was appearing over Mt. Diablo, the cold, leaden water far below, the freeway empty, the great bridge silent, deserted; and then suddenly bursting out of the tunnel a roar like the ripping of all the canvas in the west, and down he would come, all wheels broken loose on the curves as if the roadway were glass, steering with the accelerator, waving as he flashed by me at 150 miles per hour.

Charlie wanted me present on the occasion of his revenge, told me exactly where and when. I thought Heppleman should be in on it too, but couldn't find him. His answering service had no idea where he was. On a hunch I checked with the Fairmont Hotel, and sure enough he was shacked up with a blond. Discretion and admiration forbade me to bother him, even for Charlie's great moment. Charlie shot it out on Market Street in a fair fight. He accosted his brother-in-law one evening after work, threw him a gun which the bewildered man held first by the barrel; then the duel began. Like Gary Cooper, Charlie gave the villain the first shot, then cut him down. He handed over his gun to the arresting officer with an ironic bow and to me, in utter simplicity, said, "I feel a great completion. I can't describe it."

It is sad for me that these gallant men are gone, but for them one can feel no regret. They were pioneers in the wilderness of nihilism, struggling to infuse meaning into the pallid life of our times. Charlie, as you may have noticed in yesterday's *Chronicle,* has just been executed at San Quentin. His last joking words, said with a charming grin: "This is the shock treatment of thanatotherapy, guaranteed to resolve transference!" Dr. Heppleman spent two weeks with Miss Jameson then fell, or jumped, from the Fairmont Tower. His patient, by the way—this will interest you, doctor—seems to have been miraculously cured. She is appearing now as belly dancer in North Beach and is newly married to a medical student—who, by the way, is going to be a psychiatrist; so she's keeping one in the family. Six times Jimmy made it down the Waldo Grade, spinning out once and going on unperturbed. The seventh time he pushed his luck, was flat out all the way down, came out of that last corner at 180 like the pro he was, then dropped the model, the only car in history to clear the rail of the Golden Gate Bridge. He sailed 150 feet straight out in the air, even up a little, then fell slowly to the sea blowing his horn all the way down—a cry of triumph, I like to think.

And I? I who was their leader then would be their follower now if I could. I made it all possible, yet am strangely barred from their achievement. Like Moses, I led them to the promised land but cannot myself enter. What is it I lack? Why can't I *want* something?

My younger colleagues had no feeling for my new direction, thought it crazy; and I, now the only survivor of the old guard, couldn't hold them in check. They threw me out, changed the name to the American Dynamic Therapy

Association. More and more they've taken on the protective coloration of the general psychiatric establishment, retaining virtually nothing of the original insight.

I was alone then, and didn't care. Outwardly it made no difference. I would sit in my chair among things of beauty, and patients would come and I would listen; but inwardly—I hardly need tell you by now, doctor—all was changed. My newest insight had failed me, as had every other insight of my entire life. Nothing avails for long against the leeches of boredom, and they were sucking my blood again. I would sit through the day, listening as I could, and evening would come, the day's work over, and I would simply go on sitting in my decorated prison. Nothing I wanted. I had money, leisure, freedom, independence, could do anything, go anywhere. What would it be tonight? Music? Krips is playing *Das Lied von der Erde*. Art? A great Impressionist show at the De Young Museum. Books, plays, movies, night clubs, gambling, girls— everything all around. What did I want? Nothing. Not even food. Often would not go out to dinner or even to the kitchen, but sit staring at the sunset drinking gin.

Can you guess what happened next? On just such an evening? the sun sinking? . . . No? Mariette came back. Key in the lock, door opening in the dusk, and there she was, arms around me, stroking, petting, kissing, dropping hot tears on my face. "Because I love you," she said when I asked why. "And I hate you because I love you so much, can't bear thinking of you alone. What's the matter? You look so pale. I had to come back. Please be good to me."

And so she began to show me the world again. We walked through the city holding hands: "Look at the children dancing." We walked at night on the beach, arms around each other: "Look at the wake of the ship in the moonlight"; "Look at the footprints of the wind in the sand." And in bed: "Look at me. Look *at* me, not through me." But the old magic was gone. Nothing helped, the gleam in my eye grew brighter and made her sick. In the hospital I sat by her bed as she got weaker, and when she could no more than turn her head she still would say: "Look at the white clouds drifting"; "Look at the beautiful blue sky"; "Look at . . ."

. . . Sorry. For a moment I was overcome. I have a maudlin streak, you see. I'll make it brief and dry as dust. She died of course, and only then did I see the obvious: She had known, always, what had taken me a lifetime to learn; she had achieved out of greatness of heart what still was beyond me—to love something enough to risk and lose her life. I say "something," not "someone," and maybe that's my whole trouble. All along I've thought of what I sought as abstract, a principle or ideal, while she knew it was I, a particular man, whom she loved.

. . . Ah yes. "Time now," and I don't blame you. I'm telling sad tales. One more session, doctor, and we shall be finished with each other, and will both be glad. . . . My God! I hadn't seen the clock. We've run over. I'm flattered. . . . Next Friday at twelve. Fine. I'll be here. Au revoir, doctor. Pleasant weekend.

V

Good morning, doctor. Or good noon, I should say, for you're the soul of punctuality. And what a gorgeous day for our last meeting. Look! What a veil of magic has dropped from heaven on this storied city. How I love it! How truly we have honored Saint Francis to put his name to this jeweled promontory. Do you know what Mariette would say? "Look at the tiers of white houses cascading down steep hills to the glittering bay. Look at the eucalyptus trees bending in the wind, the red kites trembling over the Marina Green. Look at the white sails moving dreamlike in entranced ballet. Look!" That's what she would say. And over all—like a blessing, no, a cry of passion—the span of orange steel leaping out with matchless curves from shore to shore!

. . . Yes, I *am* manic today. From the moment I woke. I yawned, raised my arms, stretched, felt enormous vitality and happiness. How wonderful just to be, I thought. And how perfectly marvelous to be here, with this incredible beauty spread out day after day, always. Gluttonous eyes, insatiable eyes—feast! I am fortunate, I thought, beyond all dreams. There on the bed, beautiful black lover, voluptuous chambers of her body waiting for me even in sleep. And I for her! A storm of well-being flooded over me, raced through my veins, left me breathless. That's how I began my day. Make you envious?

. . . I'll tell you. It's pleasant, you know, this being a

patient. Today I canceled everything, declared a holiday.
Today I listen to no one: I speak to you. Since our last
meeting I've had another great insight, truly a revelation.
You know, doctor, the important thing about despair is
never to give up, never wrap up and put away a sterile life,
but somehow keep it open. Because you never can know
what's coming; never. That's the great thing about life,
the crucial thing to remember. You may beat your fists on
a stone wall for years and years, and every consideration of
common sense will say it's hopeless, forget it, spare youself;
and then one day your bleeding hand will go through as if
the wall were theatrical gauze; you'll be in another realm
where birds are singing and love is possible, and you'd
have missed it if you'd given up, because it might be only
that one day the wall was not stone.

So, after leaving you last week I went back for the hun-
dredth time to my stone wall. Why? Why? Why? Why was
there nothing for me? Why did my prescription work only
for others? How was I different? How come I could not do
with insight what Mariette did with intuition? Why was it
I could find nothing so desirable I would follow it to the
edge of the abyss? And all these questions were really one:
Why was there nothing I loved? And then suddenly—it was
the same unyielding spot I had hit a thousand times
before—my fist went right through. There *was* something.
I was in love with death!

A scandal, perhaps, but true. Incontrovertible the
moment it occurred to me. No wonder I could find no
death-enhanced fulfillment in something else. There *was*

nothing else. Nothing in life much interested me but death. I had, you might say, discovered death; it belonged to me, it was mine. I had defended it against all detractors, publicized it, nurtured it, sung its praises, was its priest and spokesman—poet laureate mortis. My friends could use death, instrumentally, to enhance other loves; but it was my only love, and how can death enhance itself? By dying? No, for that ends everything. My problem was how to live and yet intensify this strange love that seeks its own ending. How make this particular abstraction real without abolishing both the abstraction and its realization.

Almost at once I found the answer: death must have a symbol, a tangible form. And to my delight I found I had it already, for years, locked away in my desk lovingly wrapped in silicone cloth and velvet—a Smith and Wesson revolver, 357 Magnum. I had bought it ostensibly for protection, but it had been the companion of my boredom, not my fear, was never at my bedside to deal with intruders at night but near to hand through the slow empty days to comfort me with a reminder of the stillness that comes up to the edge of a life at beginning and end.

With a sudden vivid excitement I knew what to do. Always I had been ascetic with this gun, never played with it, touched it lightly, rarely, respectfully. But with a week to live—that was the touchstone—I'd let myself go, would take it on as a lover; I'd mount this heavy blue broad, lay hands on her, intimately, have a love affair with death. This was the answer, and like all great discoveries, once you've got it it seems easy, even obvious.

So—we began the affair. And in the usual way: we slept together. . . . You are aghast, doctor. I knew you would be. You will tell me, I think, that I have put a lethal weapon into the jittery hand of my unconscious, while I would say rather that I have surrendered myself utterly to a lover, given up all defense.

How can I tell you the delights we know? At night, my patients having gone, alone with her at last, shades drawn, the erotic scene begins. I unlock the drawer and take her out. Slowly, lasciviously, I remove her dress, strip off her lingerie, until she lies before me, shining black skin, firm flesh, unbelievably perfect curves. We begin to neck, rub each other up. I cock her, and we exchange a dizzying kiss, her muzzle in my mouth, my finger on her trigger, deliciously playing with the thought of how slight a pressure on that steel clitoris would bring us to climax.

After such a session of not quite culminated love-making I will lie panting on the bed, exhausted, utterly happy. Sighing with pleasure, arms outstretched and limp, loaded gun hanging motionless in my hand, I know I've reached my goal. The pillow under my face is an angel's breast, the softness of the bed a heavenly kindness, the moaning fog horns a delicious melody. I draw a deep breath, feel the elasticity of lungs, the strength and youth of limbs, and realize in the very depths of my being that intensification of meaning and value which is alone the true good of life.

. . . Oh yes, it's madness all right—the price I pay for integrity. Count yourself lucky, doctor, if you get it any cheaper. Faithfulness to an ideal, if carried far enough, is always madness. Only by faltering somewhere along the way, pretending not to notice, is mental health retained. . . . No, no, I don't want treatment. . . . Nor hospitalization. I appreciate your concern. You're a good listener and a good man, I feel your sympathy, but I'm content with madness. It's my contract with life, represents years of hard and honest negotiation; I wouldn't back out of it now. You must count me one of the lucky ones, a happy man.

Only one thing mars the perfection of these days: I have trouble sleeping. I used to dream vividly, violently, but now no dreams at all. A great stillness has fallen upon my armed unconscious. In fact I don't sleep, but doze lightly, hear every sound, come instantly awake at the slightest movement of my hand. Something in me doesn't trust my silent partner. But soon now. This frantic lovemaking has gone on too long. Maybe tonight we'll not make love, but lie down in each other's arms and drop off together.

There's much more I could tell you, but I'm tired, and anyway our time is up. Your next patient is waiting for you, and for me my black lover. *Buena notte.*

THE
SIGNAL

ONCE UPON A TIME
THERE WAS A MAN WHO

wanted to be a writer. Even as a child he wrote fairy
tales, which his mother thought excellent but otherwise
were not much read. In high school he yearned after
girls but was afraid of them and learned that a book, to be
significant, must have a message. As it happened he had
one: his first novel, written at seventeen in a dun-colored
YMCA room during a winter of bitter loneliness, reported that love is a bridge. In college he studied philosophy; became, in turn, a Marxist, existentialist, pacifist, and
militant organizer for SNCC; and wrote a utopia announc-
ing that narcissism is overcome by sacrifice. At a voter-
registration drive in Mississippi he met Eloise, a school
teacher from Wisconsin who seemed to know all his pas-
sions and secrets, and married her under a magnolia tree
on a day when seventeen students from Union Theological
were forced to drink castor oil and driven naked out of
Selma. Eloise was practical and strong-willed and whisked
him back to Madison where he became vice-president of

her father's cheese factory. The following year a second novel disclosed that true love dies and that loneliness, though it may have respite, has no end. "I'm not a cheese-maker," he said, "I'm a writer"; quit the business; and wrote a play in six acts called *The Road,* with a cast of forty-seven and a playing time of six hours, which made the point that seeking is better than finding. Divorced, penniless, still unpublished, he stuck with his chosen voca-tion. A poem in free verse of thirteen thousand lines asserted creativity to be the principle of life—perhaps of existence in general, for he found an analogue in the orbit of electrons, the trajectory of stars. Both his parents died of cancer; he lived alone, forgot his vitamins, became thin, and wrote a monograph declaring that creativity is in fact impossible. His name was Rainer, and he marked his works with the sign of a fox.

Everything he wrote was rejected; all his messages stayed in his trunk; and his final work—an autobiography in three volumes asserting that everything, especially the writing of books, is absurd—was not even submitted to a publisher. He himself wrote the review, found flaws, but pronounced it a masterpiece, then burned the review, the autobiography, and the trunk.

Still he lived, and ate, and one day being particularly hungry he looked through job notices and saw "Writer Wanted." What the hell, he thought, so long as it pays.

The address led him through tunnels, past factories, warehouses, across railroad tracks to a huge building with a towering chimney, a column of black smoke, a muted hum, and a curious sweet smell. A wall of blackened brick rose up from the very edge of the street, unbroken for fifty feet, to a row of tiny windows. At regular intervals gargoyles extended open mouths from the red tile roof: griffins, snakes, satyrs, dragons—all convulsed in silent, stony shrieks. There was no sidewalk; Rainer walked in the street, dodged motorcycles, looked up at the black wall, until he came to a small door. A bronze plaque announced "Mack Confections, Inc." Here the hum was louder, like a cataract deep in the earth. He hesitated, looked without purpose at his watch, glanced up the now empty street, entered.

In a dusty office he was lulled by the roar, was almost asleep when a tall, heavy man with red hair, in a pink shirt with open collar, burst into the room and attacked him with an interview. "Can you spell?" the man shouted.

"Yes."

"Spell 'fate.' " Rainer passed this test without difficulty. "All right, my boy," the man said, rubbing his beefy hands, "give us a bit of sententious wisdom. You know what 'sententious' means?"

"Yes."

"Out with it them."

The bloodshot pig-eyes were no more than three inches away; the nose was neon; the hair stood on end; the breath was pure bourbon. Rainer turned away. A torn print of Botticelli's "Birth of Venus" flapped on the dusty wall. *"Absurd!"* Rainer murmured.

"Excellent!" the man roared. "You're hired."

99

"To do what?"

"This is a fortune-cookie factory; you write the fortunes."

The man was Mr. Mack, the owner, who took Rainer into a long, high cavern of a room, past vats of flour and mixing machines. A man measuring anise raised a hand in greeting; a pretty girl pouring sugar wiped her forehead and smiled. The roar grew louder; there was a clicking and a stirring, and now a huge belt carried masses of dough between rollers; in a sheet ten feet wide the dough passed onto a conveyor of shimmering steel balls between which thousands of whirling knives suddenly rose up and cut the sheet into oval fragments that danced like leaves on a stream and flowed on into a great machine which was clicking and clacking and spewing out ribbons of green paper. High up on this machine was a dais with a keyboard, and there sat a wretched Asian darting panicky glances over his shoulder as he hunted and pecked at the keys. On the other side of the machine the leaves of dough emerged, each bearing an inch of green tape; and now, suddenly, ten thousand steel fingers reached out of the trembling stream, folded the dough over the fortunes, and gently bent them double just as the river disappeared into an oven.

Mr. Mack picked up a streamer of tape, read, and exploded. "You're fired!" he yelled, grabbing the Asian by the shirt and pulling him off the stool. Rainer looked at the tape still spewing from the machine: *Freenship is the tresur of man,* it announced, and repeated it every inch.

"You sonofabitch!" Mr. Mack yelled, shaking him, "You're ruining me. Get the hell out of here!" The man fled. Mr. Mack banged his fist on the stop button, and the press fell silent though the river of cookies still flowed. "Stop the line!" he yelled, but no one heard, and he yelled ten more times and was quite hoarse, his face purple, before the line came to rest, and the room was quiet. He mounted the dais, glared about and mopped his face with a red handkerchief.

"Now I'll show you how to do it," he said to Rainer. "C'mere. This is Tall Betsy," he said, patting the machine, "a lady and temperamental." He sat at the keyboard, extended his arms like a pianist, threw back his head and closed his eyes. A group of curious workers gathered. After a few moments succubus to the muse Mr. Mack lurched forward, typing, and the green tape sputtered forth: *Capital lies behind your eyes; invest it in the common stock of work.* "Like that," he said shyly, standing up and tearing off the tape. His face was a mixture of cunning and simplicity, of ruthlessness and sentimentality. "Only make it more goddamned interesting," he added, regaining his shouting voice. "Anybody finishing a Chinese meal is unsatisfied, but don't know what they want. *You* give it to 'em! Something to wake them up. That weak tea won't do it. *You* do it. Sit down!" Rainer sat and Mr. Mack pressed on his shoulders with both hands: "Go!" he shouted.

Rainer brushed away the hands. "Give me room," he said.

Looking out over the crowd he saw a girl of such somber

101

beauty in her wide still eyes, such store of passion in her broad soft mouth, that he felt the fish hook in his throat and the great mushroom cloud blowing up in his heart. He caught himself in time, grinned at her, turned to the keyboard and wrote: *A pretty girl is the mirage of love on the desert of loneliness. Traveler beware!* The press coughed, jerked, gave out a puff of smoke, then clickety-clacked and spewed out the tape.

Mr. Mack caught it up instantly, his lips moving as he read. "Excellent!" he roared. "Excellent!" and pressed a button marked 10,000, which directed the machine to print that many. "Hey! you peasants!" he called, throwing the tape, "Look. We got a writer!" The crowd read and laughed, all except the pretty girl who looked sad and puzzled. "Now back to work!" Mr. Mack yelled. The press clickety-clacked; the conveyor system moved; the leaves passed into the machine and emerged, each with its message of mirage; the steel fingers folded them, and into the oven they went. Mr. Mack rubbed his beefy hands. "That'll cut the taste of chow mein," he yelled, clapping Rainer on the shoulder. "Keep up the good work, my boy."

Rainer examined Tall Betsy: a typewriter keyboard, with additional keys marked "go," "stop," "hold," "protem," "1," "10," "1,000," "5,000," et cetera, up to "100,-000." So what to write? He saw children starving in India, soldiers being cut down by machine-gun fire, Jews in concentration camps, plagues, purges, inquisitions, witch hunts, and along the Appian Way an unending vista of

crucified slaves. *Tragedy is the condition of man: deny it
if you will with blindness, transcend it only with laughter.*
Tall Betsy hiccoughed; Rainer pushed the "go" button.
"The style is new," he said to the machine, "but you'll get
used to it. Give it a thousand." Now he imagined himself
an old man, dying alone in a rented room. *No second
chance; it's now or not at all.* That's worth 20,000, he
thought, and Tall Betsy seemed to agree. He laughed, I'm
going to like this job.

And indeed he did: his writing no longer *had* a message,
it *was* a message; he settled down to a pithy pessimism and
for the first time in his life began to enjoy his vocation.

The pretty girl was Delia, who added sugar to the
dough; her husband was Theo, who measured out the
anise. They were drawn to Rainer, as he to them; they invited him home, took him hiking, picnicking, to concerts.
He took them to restaurants, nightclubs, casinos; they became a trio. Delia loved birds—finches and mynahs, par-
akeets and canaries, toucans and starlings—kept hundreds
in all kinds of cages, would turn them loose on weekends,
stand in her garden in a vortex of color, a detached smile
on her face, hand raised with grain, eyes unseeing of this
world but seeing in the beating of wings some past or future, some remoteness where none could follow and she
was quite alone. Theo smoked a pipe, had a library of
Oriental religion, and was researching a life of St. Francis
as the founder of Zen. He played the recorder, warmed the

milk for the tempted cat, solved chess problems but avoided the game, studied butterflies but never put one on a
pin.

Within a few weeks after Rainer's arrival Mack Confections, Inc., was in the midst of a boom. Standing orders
were increased and new orders arrived by the hour; production was stepped up; new hands were hired. Mr. Mack
was gleeful, hopped about on one foot and then the other,
speeding up the production line, peering over his book-
keeper's shoulder, wetting his lips, shouting encourage-
ment to exhausted workers, counting his profits. The taste
of the cookies had not changed; it was the tang of the message that was making the difference. Red-and-white trucks
brought great sacks of letters praising the style and pith of
the fortunes, and quite a few, also, denouncing the author
as degenerate; people in restaurants sent compliments, not
to the chef but the writer, and three men with moustaches
sent challenges to duel. There was a sudden clamor for the
writer's name. Anonymous, Rainer became a celebrity, was
quoted by columnists, invited to address luncheons, ru-
mored to be Russian; Herb Caen said he was a Beatle.
The Pope issued a provisional excommunication, in case
he were Catholic; the D.A.R. accused him of undermining
American institutions; but the people, as Theo put it, "ate
him up." Rainer withheld his name but added the sign of
the fox to his fortunes.

The three friends would sit in restaurants and watch the
breaking of cookies and reading of fortunes. Most people
reacted as if it were their own particular lives upon which

comment was made. They would laugh, become thoughtful, embarrassed, sometimes disturbed or angry. One night
in Trader Vic's a middle-aged woman kept ordering cookies, not eating but searching as if for some particular fortune, some ray of hope perhaps; and not finding it apparently, for when she was at last led away, weeping, there was
left on the floor a pyramid of broken cookies reaching to
the table top.

Delia was fascinated, often became so curious that she
would ask of a stranger what he had read. "I don't understand it," she said one evening in a Polynesian cafeteria.
Across the room in the dim light two young heads bent
lovingly together; the woman seemed to be pleading, the
man holding back; the woman broke a cookie, read her
fortune, seemed miffed; the man read and laughed; they
left abruptly. Delia went to their table and brought back
the fortune: *In twenty minutes you will be pregnant!* "See
what trouble you make!" Delia said. Near them an old
man ate alone with palsied hands, absently slurping tea in
rheumy reverie; when finally he broke his cookie and read
the fortune he reeled as if from a blow, knocked a spoon to
the flour, shuffled across the room and out the door. Delia
went instantly to his table. *Nothing in life is certain, but
that it comes to a bad end.* "You're simply terrible!" she
said.

"In the past," Rainer said, "nothing but rejection slips;
now I write the slips, and nothing comes back. And since
reading is oral, how appropriate to publish in food."

"What are you trying to do?" Delia said, "destroy all

hope?"

"The binding is so sweet," Rainer said with a bow, "the message can afford to be bitter."

"But people can take only so much," Theo said mildly.

"I don't understand it," Delia repeated. "Why would anyone read such things?"

"If you find out," Rainer said, "why *you*, feeling as you do, read them, then you'll know."

Months passed and the Fox was famous, but declined interviews, avoided reporters, would not be photographed. When newspapermen lined up at the front door he left by the rear. Mr. Mack wanted to cash in on the notoriety, arranged interviews, television appearances, was furious at Rainer's intransigence; but made peace suddenly when it appeared that the incognito was good business. Everybody was wondering about the Fox, writing about him; his identity became a national guessing game. Mack Confections had been one of seventeen fortune-cookie factories; now there were but four, and the other three were trembling. One by one they collapsed or switched to dry cereals and comic books. The price of cookies went higher and higher, and Mack Confections became a world monopoly, supplying even Hong Kong and Peking. A staff of students translated the fortunes into forty-seven languages.

Mr. Mack became rich but refused to raise wages, said he couldn't afford it, held the union to the old contract, complained constantly about taxes and employed a staff of lawyers to be suing the government at all times. One morning after a year Rainer went into Mr. Mack's office.

"I want more money," he said.

"I don't have it, you know," Mr. Mack said nervously, wetting his lips. "The government takes every penny—you must know that, . . . don't you? Still you're a good worker. Actually I'd thought of giving you a raise—if someone works hard, is loyal, I simply want to reward him. Can't help it . . . just the kind of guy I am, I guess. So I . . . I'm going to raise you . . . to eighty-five dollars a week. How about that!" He beamed, was so touched by his generosity he began to cry.

"I want a hundred thousand a year," Rainer said, "and fifty per cent of the profits."

"You're not only crazy, you're impertinent. I won't stand it."

"Suit yourself, Mack," Rainer said, showing him a sheaf of job offers. "I can get it elsewhere. Those factories we knocked off . . . all of them want to come back to life."

So Mr. Mack gave in and Rainer took a fourteen-room penthouse on Telegraph Hill, had a cellar full of French wine, ordered suits from London, shirts from Florence, shoes from Zürich; drove a Ferrari and a Facel Vega. Hollywood wanted him in movies; he was offered a fellowship to the Center for Advanced Study in the Behavioral Sciences, invited to address the combined philosophy departments of Harvard, Yale, and Brandeis. He said no to everything, spent evenings with his two friends, would pick up a girl on his way home, come to work at noon with a yawn and a smile.

One afternoon Theo climbed Tall Betsy, lighted his

pipe, sat behind his friend. *Without security life ends in panic; without risk, in mechanization.* Rainer pushed the button marked 5,000; Tall Betsy clickety-clacked, and the green tapes wafted onto the shimmering leaves of dough. Theo laid his hand on Rainer's shoulder: "Why don't you settle down, get married?" *Pleasure is the referent of value,* Rainer wrote, and ordered a thousand. "I'm worried about you," Theo said. "A man, like a tree, needs roots. You're so detached, so alone. Too much fun, not enough love. You stand outside of life and laugh." *Truth is not enough, laughter is essential.* "You can't go on like this; something will happen." "A bolt of lightning?" Rainer asked. "You can curse God a while," Theo said, "but make a career of it . . . yes, lightning. I'm afraid for you."

"Ah Theo, you would tremble for my welfare, but it's my morals that offend you."

Another time, a warm drowsy afternoon, it was Delia who sat beside him; from the grimy skylight far above them a shaft of yellow sun, teeming with motes, fell on her golden hair. *For the experienced actor promptings of despair are cues for laughter.* "Can't you write something sweet?" Delia said. "Just once? What's the matter with you? Think it would ruin your style? Move over!" She took over the keyboard: *Love creates its own reality, and so is beyond illusion.*

"No, damn it!" Rainer said, and hit the stop button. "You'll blow the fuses. Tall Betsy is used to me, won't take those lies." He reversed the press, canceled her message, wrote, *Hope is the divining rod which dips to the sea of illusions.*

"I don't understand you," she said. "Why do you take so much away from people?" *Beware the questions of women: they say "Why?" but mean "Stop doing it!"* "Don't make fun of me," Delia said, suddenly pleading. "I'm your friend, am terribly fond of you. I simply want to understand you." Rainer kissed her, swung back to the keyboard: *Beware the woman who wants to understand you; she understands you already, wants now to change you.* "You're simply terrible," Delia said.

Once it happened that Theo was away, and Delia and Rainer spent a day together, swam in the ocean, waltzed on tile parquetry under the moon, drank tequila in a flamenco cellar, and when they got home Delia wouldn't stop, put on a record of Edith Piaf, brought out champagne. She threw open the cages, and the birds flew screeching around her head. "Come dance with me," she said, but he refused. "Is Don Juan of the cookie factory worn out from his conquests? No more zip, eh?" She kicked off her shoes and danced with the circling birds, round and round in a flashing vortex of feathers, spilling champagne, pulling up her dress for high kicks, until suddenly she collapsed.

She woke to a terrible stab of guilt but found she was fully dressed, covered with blankets; Rainer had put the birds in their cages, turned off the lights, and gone home. She got up with a hangover, but happy, and went to work; Rainer waved from his dais, and she smiled. In the afternoon she climbed up beside him. "I'm so happy," she said, "and so grateful. You're not the opportunist you pretend to be. You put loyalty above pleasure . . . or you would have stayed last night."

"You're mixed up, sweetie. You were fiercely seductive, and I wanted to stay, you're right about that. But wrong about everything else. I put nothing above pleasure. The greater pleasure is simply with the three of us, the fun we have. No sacrifice. Sorry, . . . I mean no slight to your considerable charms." *Faced with incompatible pleasures, choose the keener.*

In time Mr. Mack became the seventh wealthiest man in the world, lived in a castle with a moat, had thirteen servants, one wife, two children, three mistresses; but was not happy. He became ever more irritable, fumed about the production line, complaining, scolding, losing his temper. "Oh you blockhead!" he said to Theo one day, "that's too much anise. How long've you been on this job? . . . My God! You're fired. Get the hell outa here," and in an upsurge of petulance slapped Theo in the face. "You're overwrought," Theo said, "better rest a bit." "None of your lip, young man!" Mr. Mack said, slapping him again. "I'll have your skin."

"What's the matter with Mack?" Theo asked Rainer. "Bad conscience," Rainer said. "He doesn't look well," Theo said; "I worry about him." "Well, don't," Rainer said, and wrote: *Bastards need to suffer; it helps them stand themselves.*

Bad luck befell Mr. Mack. Mrs. Mack left him, tied up the community property with injunctions, estranged their daughter. His teen-age son, driving drunk, had a head-on collision, suffered a broken back, killed the other driver. A disaffected worker with a shotgun left pellets in Mr. Mack's lung, powder burns on his face. He became thin, pale, explosive. Only to Theo did he feel close: he hung around the anise station, listened as Theo talked of poetry and philosophy, and sometimes became calm, showed human feeling.

He fell sick, was hospitalized. His son died; his wife and daughter would not visit him. He was found to have a malignant anemia and to be of a blood type so rare that no donor could be located. He issued an appeal to his workers, but few came forward; he was about to die when Theo was discovered to be of the same type and offered blood. This indebted Mr. Mack, and he became even more nasty, sarcastic. Delia visited him once and was showered with obscenity; his workers were eager for his death; he had no friends but Theo. The doctors said it was hopeless, but every day Theo would sit at his bedside, spoon-feed him, hold his hand, suffer his insults, give him hope.

Though Delia protested, two or three times a week Theo would give a transfusion. She asked Rainer to intervene. "What's this blood relationship?" Rainer asked Theo. "Why so wrapped up in the boss?"

"It's not the disease that's killing him," Theo said, "but his own hatred. He can't believe in love, so keeps proving to himself that no one can love him by being so mean that no one will."

"A son of a bitch, in other words. How does it concern you?"

"Maybe I can show him the reality of love."

"You're a fool, Theo; you're playing Christ. There are better roles, certainly less pretentious."

The transfusions did not help; Mr. Mack grew weaker, thinner, and one day Theo saw that he was dying. His flesh was yellow; he could not turn his head; only his eyes moved, and directed at Theo a baleful gaze. He seemed to want to speak, and Theo brought his ear close to the waxen lips. "Dying is bad enough," Mr. Mack whispered; "it's too much, in addition, to see your stupid face. Get from here and be damned and don't come back."

Theo looked at him a long moment then sat beside him, took his hand. "You don't mean that, Mr. Mack; I'm not going to leave you, and you're not going to die. You will get well. Believe me. Trust me." Their eyes locked in struggle. After a while Mr. Mack seemed to surrender; hatred drained from his gaze; his face relaxed; he turned his cheek to the pillow and slept.

Now Theo was ill, almost as pale as Mr. Mack, his bones shaken by a sudden fever. The nurses put him to bed in Mr. Mack's room; Delia and Rainer kept watch, one of them always there. Delia wept, scolded, cajoled, but could not reach him. His eyes became luminous; his flesh dissolved; and on the third day he seemed not so much to die as to go to Heaven. Delia and Rainer walked away dry-eyed, abandoned. "I wish he had waited for me," Delia said.

Three weeks later Mr. Mack left the hospital; a month later he was back at work—thin, quiet, ghostlike. As his strength returned he began to move about the factory, walk along the production line. Sometimes Delia would look up to find him staring at her from a dark corner, eyes brimming with tears. Often he mounted the dais and sat absently behind Rainer.

One day he called Delia into his office, with elaborate courtesy sat her down, started to speak; he swallowed, walked about, wiped his eyes, cleared his throat, planted himself before her. "Your husband, . . . my dear girl, . . . Theo, . . . a great man, very great man. Never did it occur to me"—with the beginning of rhetoric he seemed to recover a bit—"that a truly great man would work here, in my factory, under this roof, measuring out the anise." He gazed at her hungrily, stroked the back of her hand, burst into tears. "My dear girl, I . . . am settling his salary upon you in permanent trust."

"Well bully for him!" Rainer said when Delia told him. "I'm not surprised about the tears, but am astonished they dissolve the glue that sticks him to money."

One morning Rainer found the bronze plaque replaced, the new one identifying the company as "Theobald Cookies, Inc." All the stationery had been changed, all the signs, and a long eulogy of Theo mailed to all customers. Mr. Mack hung about Delia that day, beaming, but she was embarrassed and could say nothing. He went then to Rainer who gave him a sardonic stare: "What do you want, old boy, a pat on the head?" Mr. Mack suggested a series of fortunes dedicated to Theo: "I want every man who breaks a cookie, anywhere in the world, to think of Theo." Rainer exploded: "You shovel the sentiment, Mack; leave the fortunes to me." *The guilt of the quick raises monuments to the dead.* Mr. Mack turned away, crestfallen.

One Monday morning at eleven the alarm sounded, the production line stopped, and over the loud speakers came Mr. Mack's funereal voice: "All hands stand by at the fortune press." He arrived with head bowed, hands clasped behind his back; mounted the dais, faced the crowd, and slowly raised his arms high and wide as if to embrace them all. For a long minute he held this pose. "We are gathered together," he said finally, "to honor the memory of our dear departed—fellow worker, loyal friend, dearly beloved, . . ." his voice broke, ". . . now lost to us. Let us bow our heads in prayer." Nothing could be heard in the great room but a faint whispering of wind high up in the skylight. "All of us," Mr. Mack continued, "have been grieving alone in our hearts. It will draw us closer if we share our grief and memories. Theo would have wanted this. I call first on Theo's best friend, our great writer."

Mr. Mack stepped aside, hands piously folded. Rainer looked out over the crowd; three men in the front row were crying. For a moment he hesitated, then stepped lightly to the edge of the platform.

"Not much to say. Theo was born in 1923, had few talents, an undistinguished life; pretensions to scholarship but a limited mind. He liked to sing, loved Scotch whisky, had a great eye for the pretty ankle—but was inhibited, guilty, would seldom look at a pretty knee. He was a fool, too, and died from giving too much blood. A gentle man, with a shy smile, a good friend. I'm sorry he's gone.

"But you do him no honor with these tears. It's not grief you feel, nor even loss, but self-pity. You weep for yourselves."

There was a murmur of outrage; Mr. Mack leapt to his feet. "I protest! In the name of his wife, friends, fellow workers . . . in the name of us all I repudiate this description." Rainer shrugged, sat down. "Theo was a simple man, to be sure," Mr. Mack continued, "but in the way of Jesus. He was truly a Christ among us, and no one shall defame him." He turned to glare at Rainer. "The idea of sacrifice," he went on, "is the fountainhead of morality; without it we are beasts in the jungle. But we must not take it for granted. It could be lost. It has lived from Calvary to this moment only because a few gallant, selfless spirits have embodied it at the cost of their own lives. Theo was one such, and we are blessed to have known him, honored to have heard his voice, touched his hand. We must enshrine his example in our spirits, labor to become worthy." He raised his arms. "Go now in peace, and may his grace be with you."

"I hand it to you, Mack," Rainer said as the crowd dispersed. "There was many a moist eye, many a drippy nose. Can you kiss babies too? . . . You ought to run for governor." Mr. Mack, descending Tall Betsy with clerical step, did not deign to reply.

That week Rainer wrote of morality:

> *The idea of sacrifice disguises the hope of saving one's own skin.*
>
> *Herd animals may be identified by the tendency to carry Bibles.*
>
> *Morals are the distillate of security operations.*

On Tuesday there were mutterings against him in the toilet; on Wednesday a petition to fire him was circulated; on Thursday as he left the factory five-hundred workers standing in a straight line stared in silent denunciation. On Friday when he arrived, Mr. Mack was standing on Tall Betsy before a crowd of workers, apparently having just finished a speech.

"I shall now myself write a fortune," Mr. Mack said, casting a nervous glance at Rainer. "In memory of Theo it will be disseminated in our famous confection throughout the world." He sat at the keyboard, speaking as he wrote: *Greater love than this hath no man, that he lay down his life for his friend.* There was a chorus of approbation, a few amens. Rainer leapt to the dais and hit the stop key. "Not over my mark," he said and, reaching into the machine, withdrew the sign of the fox. Mr. Mack then pressed the key that called for 100,000 copies. The machine sputtered, jerked. "You'll choke Betsy on that stuff," Rainer said, but presently the machine acquiesced, began the familiar clickety-clacking. Mr. Mack held aloft the tape. "The mark of the beast is gone," he said. "The essence of Christ remains."

On Monday Rainer again found Mr. Mack at Tall Betsy, writing, but no crowd this time. As Rainer started to mount the dais his way was blocked by Robert Farley, six feet four, two-hundred-ninety pounds. Farley was an ex-machinist, ex-musician, whose job was to sharpen the thousand knives which cut the dough into cookie-size leaves. He was a sentimental giant easily moved to tears, had served a term for manslaughter a few years back, having done in his wife with a butcher knife and tried to ship her out of the country, dismembered, in a cello case. Right now his eyes were red from crying, his shirt wet on either side of his chest where tears had dropped unnoticed. His face was contorted, his lips moved silently.

"What's with you, Farley?"

Farley stuttered, raised his arms, inarticulate, presently took the tape issuing from the machine, put it in Rainer's hand: *He that findeth his life shall lose it: and he that loseth his life for my sake shall find it.* Farley jabbed his fingers at this message several times, then gasped: "You . . . don't . . . write . . . any . . . more."

"Idiot!" Rainer said. "Out of my way."

"Don't push your luck, buddy." With the approach of violence Farley regained ease and voice.

117

Rainer grabbed his shirt and gave a shove, which had no effect; whereupon Farley with an easy swipe of his left arm knocked Rainer flat, sent him sliding ten feet on the floor. Rainer got to his feet, grabbed a twelve-pound spoon, and had started for Farley when Mr. Mack jumped down between them. "Hold it, Rainer. A word with you please." He took Rainer's arm, drew him away. "Don't antagonize him," Mr. Mack said gently. "Come, walk with me. You and Farley must learn to love each other."

"You've flipped, boss. You got a psychiatrist?"

Mr. Mack gave a false and priestly chuckle, threw an arm lightly over Rainer's shoulder. "Some of the boys have been moved to express in writing their admiration for Theo, as is fitting and proper. So for a while, perhaps, . . . they will write the fortunes and you may . . . be relieved. Farley will lead off."

"But Farley is stupid!"

"He's devout. Intelligence is not everything."

"For a writer," Rainer said, "nothing can take the place of intelligence."

"Well there may be some little difference of opinion about that. Why don't you take a vacation. Get some rest. Meditate a bit; remember the past; think about Theo. It'll do you good . . . may help you understand what we're doing here."

They walked back to the press where Farley was now installed, his great hulking shape dwarfing the keyboard, darting uneasy glances here and there with his small tearful eyes. Rainer picked up the tape: *Blessed are the poor in spirit: for theirs is the kingdom of heaven.*

"But perhaps you should give me back that little fox-sign," Mr. Mack said. "Our customers seem to expect it."

"No dice, Mack. You can print the Bible verse by verse, but not over my mark."

For several days, in millions of cookies, Farley gave his thoughts to the world:

> *All of us are guilty; the only redemption is sacri-fice.*
> *So long as anyone in the world is dying all are guilty.*
> *He that is without sin among you, let him first cast a stone.*
> *You are your brother's keeper and your brother is everywhere.*

On the fourth day he gave up all pretense of invention and, with Bible open before him, began pecking out the Gospel according to Matthew, and was quickly replaced; but not before seventeen carloads of cookies had been stuffed with the genealogy of Christ (*And Aram begat Aminadab—Ezekias begat Manasses—and Zorababel begat Abiud*) and had to be destroyed.

The next writer was Hartfell, the baker, huge, pasty-faced, dressed in white, and covered altogether, even his eyelashes, with a fine dust of flour. He did not so much sit on Tall Betsy as hover above her like a cloud. He was a philosopher, much concerned with the definition of man:

Cunning, perception, even foresight, all these we share with beasts; only sacrifice makes the man.

Some beasts look like men, talk like men, act more or less like men; but if they have not a willingness to sacrifice they are of the jungle.

Brevity was not within his compass. He grew quickly so verbose, even by the end of the first day, that his fortunes were running to three paragraphs; the folding mechanism was wrapping the cookies in the fortunes instead of the other way round, while from the oven came the acrid smoke of burning paper.

There was however no dearth of replacements. Secretly everybody was a writer, and there followed a succession of workers each presiding for a while on the dais pecking out favorite aphorisms, cherished platitudes, homespun insights. Tall Betsy had frequent breakdowns, blowing fuses, shorting out, giving off noxious fumes, occasionally even sent an electric shock into the seat of a writer. Mr. Mack thrived on the regime of piety, regained his rotund contour. In his face the lines of suffering faded, leaving only the guise of guilt.

Rainer no longer cared nor spent much time in the factory. Occasionally he would wander in, read the tape, wave ironically to the sweating, lip-moving writer, walk along the production line, flirt with the girls. In an atmosphere of reverence he was inclined to make jokes, to whistle, and one Thursday was come upon in the spice room stretched out with a laughing redhead.

"Cut down on the sugar," he told Delia; "they're putting so much in the fortunes you don't need it here." She was offended that he would not grieve for Theo, but he was unmoved. No time for that, he told her; sorry. She was lonely, he talked to her, and after a while she became less angry. He played with her birds, told funny stories, took her out in the evenings, and a time came eventually when he stayed the night.

One day as Rainer entered the factory Mr. Mack was lurking in the hallway. "Good morning, son, how are you? Come in my office . . . sit here. This chair is more comfortable. Cigar?"

"What's the matter, Mack? You look worried."

"Well, I am . . . about you." He admitted this with a rueful boyish honesty and bit off the end of a cigar. "Fact is I've never felt quite right about . . . putting you on forced leave, as it were. Oh it was my own doing, I'm the first to admit that. But it was not quite fair—I see that now. Anybody can make a mistake; I guess that's just the way we mortals are. But we have to make amends. So, I just want to say to you, man to man, 'I'm sorry,' and I'm giving you back your job."

"I don't believe you, Mack. Anyway I'm used to not working now, I like it."

Mr. Mack became reflective, took a different tack. "You know, Rainer, there's a lot of feeling against you, and it's bound to get worse. The men resent your getting paid without working. There was an attempt on my life, you know. The same could happen to you. Frankly I'm worried."

"You're cracking my heart wide open. What's that under your hand?" Rainer seized a folder that Mr. Mack was trying to hide, and in the tussle there fell to the floor a chart of sales which showed a precipitous drop. Rainer grinned: "Looks like a ski jump." Along with the chart was a sheaf of letters demanding the return of the Fox. "So that's it," Rainer said. "Ah Mack, was it just a good-time morality? Is it not also for adversity?" "None of your lip, young man!" "Would you, for mere money," Rainer went on, "call back a writer whose principles you deplore? How crass of you!"

Mr. Mack himself began the writing of fortunes, dredging from ancient depths fragments of Benjamin Franklin and Horatio Alger, but could achieve no zip or tang, and every mail brought cancellations of orders. He tried then to copy Rainer's cynicism (*Life ends!—Check in your suit! —Meet you on the bridge!*) but people heard the phony note and were bored. He forged the sign of the fox, but no one was fooled. Other factories reëntered the field. Again he begged Rainer to write, offered a bonus, a larger share of profits. "Absolutely not," said Rainer. Mr. Mack hired one writer after another, firing them in quick succession; he brought Hartwell back for a while, even Farley. Nothing was left now of Mr. Mack's clerical manner: he strode along the production line, occasionally cuffing a worker, hovered about Tall Betsy, yelled at his writers, called them peasants, buffoons, and soon no one would write. He had to do it himself, would sit at the keyboard, sweat and swear and pound his head. His blood pressure rose, the rest of his hair fell out, his temper was extremely bad.

The company was now foundering. Wages were lowered; every week hundreds of employees were laid off. The great room was poisoned by an atmosphere of distrust, recrimination; workers went about with lowered heads and sullen faces, muttered in the locker rooms, beat their wives at home. One day, as it occurred to Mr. Mack that a woman might have the knack for fortunes, he assigned the job to Delia. "I don't want it," she said. "Do it or get out," he said. Already her wages had been cut, the trust revoked; she could hardly buy food for her birds. So she sat on Tall Betsy and wrote from her heart:

> *The maze of love is better than all straight roads.*
> *Better to live in the street and be jostled than alone in a tower of gold.*
> *No victory over death but a tangle of loving hearts.*

Mr. Mack was enthusiastic at first—"Excellent!" he declared, "pure beauty, pure poetry!"—but cookie-eaters of the world were not impressed and sales continued to drop. Writing became for Delia a heavy burden, sometimes made her frantic. Often Rainer would sit with her on Tall Betsy, teasing a bit, petting her, playing with her hair.

Mr. Mack was enraged at his bad luck, scapegoated everybody. Customers no longer complained; they had lost interest in a failing concern, simply placed their orders elsewhere. Delia felt the continuing failure now as her responsibility, wanted desperately to stop, but Mr. Mack had no one else and would not permit it. One day when she went to his office to plead he pulled her on his lap, thrust a hand between her thighs, and when she slapped him said, "I can't meet the payroll, may have to let you go—unless you are nice to me."

Wages were cut a second time and then a third. The union charged bad faith, claimed that Mr. Mack's personal fortune was still in the hundreds of millions, pointed out that stock dividends had not been cut. A strike was announced but was called off when a spy reported that Mr. Mack wanted the strike as pretext for a shutdown. The union filed suit for breach of contract; Mr. Mack retaliated with another wage cut; the union filed for an injunction.

Rainer was aloof from it all, busy in pleasure; days would pass without his coming in. He drew an undiminished salary; Mr. Mack was afraid to fire him. One afternoon, having been away for a week, he climbed the dais with a huge bouquet of yellow chrysanthemums. Delia smiled as he kissed her, forced herself to look at the flowers, but her face was drawn and distant; her eyes avoided his. He looked at the tape:

He who seeks certainty in ideas is lost finally in experience.

Anger makes barriers, stops the flow of life.

124

A fool may find love, but only the wise and brave can hold it.

He tried to cheer her, told her of travels and encounters, and when still he could not reach her went away and returned with a humming bird, yellow and blue, in a silver cage. Delia looked at the bird for a long time, then opened the cage, held the gram of life in her hand. Abruptly she set it free and turned back to her work, not even looking to see where it had flown. Rainer put his hands on her shoulders, stroked her neck and hair. *Oh sweetheart,* she wrote, *why couldn't we have found each other a long time ago? Before it was too late?* She began to cry; he turned her to him. "I can't go on," she sobbed, suddenly flung herself in his arms, burrowing her wet face in his shoulder. "Such a beautiful bird!" she cried, "but it would die with me. I can't make them happy; they don't sing any more. They sit in their cages and look at me and are sad. I can't stand the way I live. Mr. Mack offers money if I spy on the union; the union wants me to sleep with Mr. Mack, get something on him. Oh I hate them all and I can't write fortunes and I loathe this job!"

Rainer held her until she was calm, looked keenly in her face, then took her seat at the keyboard, pulled up his sleeves, put the sign of the fox in the machine. "Now cheer up," he said, and wrote:

Humor is a luxury to happiness, a necessity to despair.

He that is without sadness among you, let him first cast a stone.

Security is reciprocal to change.

Animals should work; the duty of man is pleasure; sacrifice is for saints.

Tall Betsy seemed to recognize the touch; the clickety-clacking grew faster, smoother, took on a syncopated rhythm and a kind of purring. A few curious workers gathered to watch; Mr. Mack appeared with his body-guard, picked up the tape. "Excellent!" he roared, "excellent! That'll cut the taste of soy sauce. Now back to work you peasants. Speed up the line. We got a writer."

With the first new shipment orders began pouring in. The Fox was remembered; arguments sprang up about him; columnists quoted him; again there was the clamor for interviews. As sales increased, Mr. Mack raised the price and hired more workers; once again rival companies were forced into receivership or the production of bubble-gum and comic books. Feature stories about the Fox appeared in magazines; he was known as the "Destroyer of Transcendence" and "Founder of the Cult of the Present"; college students wrote term papers about him; a collection of his fortunes was published, under the title *Adventures in Nihilism,* in a paperback series on living philosophers. His were the first fortune cookies ever to be copyrighted, occasioning a debate in Washington as to whether whole cookies or just the messages should be deposited in the Library of Congress. (The Department of

Copyrights considered the pastry as a binding and wanted whole cookies; the Section on Pests of the Department of Health, Education and Welfare said this would bring roaches to the stacks and was a hazard to health.) He became more famous and more wealthy, but remained anonymous. He built a Porsche Spyder and drove in road races, learned Spanish and bought a ranch in Mexico, collected Mayan art and Persian wall hangings. Two or three times a week he came to the factory to write fortunes; when away for any length of time he cabled them to Delia who fed them to Tall Betsy. He played polo in Nassau, sailed a twenty-eight-foot sloop around the Horn alone, bought a topless nightclub and personally interviewed each applicant.

One afternoon in July when the air was hot and still Delia knelt behind him as he worked, arms around his neck, ruffling his hair, murmuring in his ear. From the high skylight a shaft of golden, mote-loaded sunlight fell on the dais, enveloped them both. Suddenly down through the pillar of light with a delicate beating of wings swooped a humming bird, yellow and blue, and seized the tape issuing from Tall Betsy. Delia cried out in delight, "Oh look! It's come back. It's our own." The bird tugged in vain at the tape, dropped it, swooped down to the moving production line to take a fortune from one of the cookies, and there, caught by the foot in the folding mechanism, fluttered helplessly. Rainer leaned out to get it, could not, leaned further, slipped, fell across the river of trembling leaves. As he started to rise ten thousand steel fingers reached up seized his clothes and flesh. He struggled for a minute, then knew it was hopeless. With his left arm, which was all he could move, he freed the bird. Delia screamed unheard; the production line moved on; Rainer looked up with a smile and a wave and was carried into the oven to his death. The bird fled upward through the golden shaft with Rainer's last fortune: *Don't cry for help; there is no help; but give a signal.*

Meditations

T O
B E
A
G O D

AMONG THE FIRST TO

ARRIVE, WE CLIMB TO

a bench beneath a tree. Beside us over a low stone wall the
vineyard falls away across the hillside. Gnarled vines ud-
dered with grape, evenly spaced and pruned, manacled
each to its low frame, descend in long green lines. Among
them move a horse and plowman, slowly, with unsure foot-
ing, the red earth turning between the vines, plowshare
flashing in the sun. In the grass along the wall a column of
ants; on stage two young men arranging chairs for the
string orchestra. The sun is past the zenith, throws a pattern of leaves on my wife's bent head. To the west a tidal
wave of fog spills over the coastal hills, is burned by sun to
incandescence. To the east, down-sloping fields, a line of
trees and a ravine, another vineyard, a meadow and more
trees, and the level valley floor, cities and towns, the freeway like an ant trail, the silver bay, the far mountains,
summer . . . the blue sky over all!

My summer too, far enough along to see the end: work a
little harder, make more money, children off to college,

freedom then and the world tour, back and more work, weddings and thrown bouquets, and then the coronary. Is this the way to live? Who knows the question knows not how; who knows not the question cannot tell.

The amphitheater is being filled: a chatter of voices, a false laugh, chic women in spike heels and beehive coiffures crowding up the grassy path. How do others live? The musicians settle themselves on the stage with a clatter of chairs, begin the tuning of instruments. Around us gray-haired men with white handkerchiefs bend gravely and dust benches; young women in sundresses, with firm brown arms, glance at each other, compare clothes, compare . . . compare. There's Arthur Lapham with a flaming redhead, looking over her to all who enter, nodding, waving, ready always for the big chance. And Dr. Naser-hof, psychoanalyst with the sad yellow face, shoulders stooped as if by an invisible weight, a tall spare frame that lay stretched on my couch (for I too am an analyst), feet dangling, four times a week for—how many?—years; for a while analysis itself becoming for him the meaning of life, a kind of formal minuet in which the learning of new psychic steps replaced lost illusions; with insight to spare but no change, coming in time to feel betrayed, but still on the couch for years . . . years, creating for my ears elegies of transience and disillusion, laments on the wandering restlessness of man—saying, "I came to this hospital as a resident and still remember how it was. And how I was. Patients would arrive sick and leave well. Something would happen—insight—that made a difference. So I thought. It's the same now; but I'm different, and what they achieve is respite, not change. For any significant change proves illusory, and any real change proves insignificant. Whatever was wrong with them stays wrong, recurs, the same or slightly different, and they muddle along for a while with ups and downs and then come back. And the second time is like the first—some new insights, some new 'realizations,' some new 'turning points'—like the wind turns"; —now, himself behind the couch, making fifty thousand a year, his heart still feeling the sterility of life, great gifts going to waste, wanting to give himself to something—research perhaps, or teaching, maybe the Peace Corps—but can't be sure, putting it off, never deciding, moving meanwhile from wife to wife, coming back to see me at his third divorce (that young woman on his arm with the tight dress and plunging neckline, is she number four?), hesitating at the door, vaguely touching the books with his long fingers, saying, "I read a little Tillich . . . very good . . . very stimulating . . . try to find out something, some meaning . . . the style is difficult. . . ." Prisoner of the past . . . could he choose a different life? Could I?

Before my eyes, high in the sky appear two moving white lines. The aircraft are invisible, the vapor trails appearing as the writing of white chalk on blue slate. I think of it as a message from a distant communicant and try to read, but the graceful curves fade too quickly. I imagine myself then at the site of these aircraft, giddy in the thin air, see the gleaming metal, am deafened by the roar of wind and motor; enter the cockpit, see the oxygen mask over the young face, the full lips, the steady eyes—and remember, suddenly, an experience swimming at La Jolla. I had gone down twelve feet in clear water and there, by the rocks, had rolled over and looked up. At the surface, glittering in the sun, two silver fish had flashed by.

I sit here now and look up from the floor of an ocean of air. In a billion years life has lifted itself from the bottom of the sea to the surface and then onto land; moves upward now in this more rare ocean; and up there at this moment, beyond my vision, are two frolicking fish who have reached the very surface, chasing each other and splashing about, and one day may leap out entirely, into an even freer realm.

The planes have disappeared now; the vapor trails vanish. I know not those pilots, will never see their faces, and what matters it to me or to them that for a moment they came within my vision? There was perhaps a moment in time, a billion years ago, when a sluggish monster rolling at the bottom of a murky sea looked up and chanced to see some more agile creatures rising toward the surface. What could that rudimentary brain have known of the life to come, and what care I now for that ancient moment of dull perception? And what will it matter one day to creatures who will live and think in ways unimaginable to me that a billion years back I—who am I?—should have sat here on a March day on the floor of this ocean and looked up and seen those metal fish flash by and that somehow to this dull brain there came the intimation of a freer life?

Near the stage I see my friend Simon; the place is full of psychoanalysts. He raises a hand in greeting, starts up the grassy path—a barrel of a man with a rolling walk, sun gleaming on bald head, a bristling moustache, swarthy skin with genial wrinkles, black eyes darting furiously, mouth working over a black cigar, rolling it, chewing it, issuing billows of smoke as if for a festival. I know from his manner he has something to tell me. "C'mere," he says, plucking my arm, and leads me some distance away from possible interruption; "got a gem for you." He backs me against a tree, puffs harder in anticipation of brief abstinence, explodes in smoke shrouding us both. "Listen to this!" He puts the cigar on a branch near my head, fixes me with restless tormented eyes, and pokes me lightly on the chest to prevent my attention from wandering. "This happened yesterday in a supervision hour . . . candidate reporting on the analysis of a thirty-seven year old man. The patient remembered something from early childhood: he had waked at night with an earache and called for his mother. She came in her nightgown, took his temperature, and said he had to have medicine. He cried; she insisted. When she went to get the medicine he got out of bed, ran silently down the hall to his parents' bedroom, and slipped in beside his sleeping father. When the medicine was prepared his mother couldn't find him. . . . O.K.? Understand? That's the memory. At that point I interrupted the candidate: 'Stop right there,' I said; 'I will predict for you the content of the next hour!' "

Simon pauses, and I register an obliging astonishment. "So . . . ?" he says, poking me a little harder with the stubby forefinger, ". . . what did I tell him?" Having long since given up these psychoanalytic puzzles, along with three-move chess problems, I shrug in amiable defeat. "It's easy," Simon says. " 'The patient will stand up his wife and try to seduce his analyst.' The candidate's mouth fell open when I said that—because that's exactly what had happened. In the very next hour the patient reported having forgotten to meet his wife, left her standing on Union Square; she was furious. And in that same hour, at the end, when he got up from the couch—whatdya think?—he gave the candidate a stock tip: 'Buy Sundown Oil,' he said. 'It's a sleeper; there's going to be a sellout. It'll double at least.' Get it?" Simon shouts, the finger jabbing gleefully. "Get it? *'Sleeper'! 'Sellout'!* Isn't that beautiful! Isn't that a gem!" A few more exclamations, and the story is over. I rejoin my wife, furtively rubbing my chest. Simon wanders off, billowing smoke again, hails a friend, launches into another story.

And the others here around me . . . how do they live? On a Sunday afternoon like this they drive out of the city into hills and meadows, in sunlight, to a concert; and tomorrow will wake and dress and eat, go to work; will sell houses, buy stock, examine patients, teach classes, settle estates, look after children; then home to the two cocktails

and dinner, then the movie or committee meeting or television or party, and more to drink and so to bed and the
making of love—with love or without—and to sleep, the
earth turning, the sun rising, and so all again. And all this
is perhaps nothing of choice, no creation, but the life
process as given—to this species in this time and place—
a role we play with a make-believe of independence, but
then we die for real.

And I? The same: ten patients a day now, make more
money, pay more taxes, buy more stocks and better
clothes, drink more wine, worry about practice, reputation, Russians, cholesterol . . . the same old things. Is
this the way to live? Is there a choice?

The cacophony of tuning dwindles, ends; the conductor
enters to applause; the hush, the raised baton, the poised
bows; then a lyric soaring light as a butterfly, deft as a
humming bird, and, oh, I wish I had lived in the time of
that music. That's the harmony of the spheres, Boccherini
plucked it out of the air. That's the Heavenly City being
erected on Europe's green and pleasant land. That's the
graceful motion of infinitely perfectible man, the serene
processional on the path of progress. That's the eighteenth
century. Never before or since has man achieved such an
orderly image of life. Maybe I would have been stifled by
its smugness, but I envy its certainties. When one is so sure
one can afford to be good. We are in the slough of doubt;
it has a bitter taste and a discordant sound.

The audience is still now, faces fixed on the stage like a
bed of strange flowers combed by the wind. The bows

move in unison, while above us the leaves of poplar turn simultaneously at the touch of inaudible breeze; we are caught and held by a pattern of notes from the eighteenth century and are caught up beyond this music in something not of our choosing, a solemn procession, living out' assigned roles, disappearing like leaves. Choice? Where is choice? We look like gods but are like that horse, in invisible harness, pulling an invisible plow, obediently, day after day, down the same furrow to the same end.

It is easy to admit to this malaise if one is willing to label it sickness—middle age depression, perhaps, or involutional state. Life is not impugned. One may go then to an analyst for help, may even speak of it to friends. But those who regard it as the stuff of which our days are made cannot speak. When truth means despair we seek illusion, and who dare attack such a choice?—who, indeed, other than those who covet the freedom to make it. We cannot, having no other life to offer, betray the life that betrays us. I too have been silent, speak now only because—sitting here in this pleasant company on this sunny afternoon, feeling days run through me and on like an unknowable river, seeing my image in that horse and plowman—I am again in search of a freedom beyond constraint. How came I here, to this point in the furrow? Who am I?

I understand the Pharaohs. I too would build a monument against time. It goes far back in my life. I used not a knife but a hatchet to cut my initials in an elm tree; cut deep, in letters a foot high; it took hours. But after a year or two the edges rolled; the shapes twisted; the letters disappeared in scar. I would read Dostoevski, feel moved, exalted, grateful, but couldn't leave it at that, would put myself in his place and think, "If I had written these novels I would be remembered by others as he is now remembered by me," and so began a straining after immortality with a pen.

I hated work that has to be done over: washing dishes, sweeping floors, paying bills. As a boy I had to chop weeds between rows of corn; all spring and summer they would grow and I'd chop them, and always they grew back. I never finished. So little time to shape a permanence, and this was wasting it; and as I grew older I avoided or minimized everything that gets repeated—writing letters, even eating. It's quicker to get a hamburger at the joint on the corner, to stand up and wolf it down, than to sit at a table set with linen and silver and crystal. The hunger for immortality makes food plain. I had no flowers; they have to be watered, fertilized, pruned, and put in the sun, and whatever you do to them you have to do again; you're never through. Houses have to be painted, roofs patched, plumbing fixed, furnaces cleaned; I lived in furnished rooms. Pets have to be fed and walked and taken to the vet; I had none. Friendships too have to be looked after; so mine were few. My wish to live forever was in a fair way of preventing me from living at all. The sacrifice upon which talent was to flourish was starving any talent I may have had.

But in the long run even that didn't matter; for I came to feel that I was not a free but a driven agent and that the drive was hopeless, that no art is beyond time. I don't read Aeschylus or Dante, hardly read Shakespeare. As literature becomes more distant it becomes more alien, has less to say to us. It dies too. There's some kind of pain. . . . It changes, no definition holds it, but some kind of pain, death perhaps—however far away coming closer—the lack of meaning—something. Whatever it is, it's a goad. It won't let me stop, makes me grope again, stirs up the old hope, and off I go. Then the whole thing starts over. I've been through it many times.

Marxism was another round. I catch a glimpse in Marx of what I'm after, seize on it, pursue it, study, work, think. The system takes shape, illumines life, gives meaning to history, makes sense of everything. I believe in it; it's a rock; I cling to it; I *know* it's true. But years pass, and nothing happens, and finally I turn on it and tear it apart. It's phony as a sideshow, riddled with wish and assumption, not a liberation but a cross. And all this may be valid, this attack, but is nevertheless a blind; for it was not desire for the social good that drove me, and the bitterness came not from the error of Marxism, but from something obscure, personal—still there, unaffected, mysterious.

But I can't just stop, I get restless, begin to brood. In us, around us, is the emptiness out of which we came, toward which we're tending. Something gnaws on me; time is passing, wasting, and something I ought to be doing, some mystery slipping through my fingers, something precious.

So I look, and what I see is something I already knew and tried to forget. The mystery is life . . . and the something precious . . . and it *is* slipping away. So what to do? Suicide I rule out; resignation is not my style. A life that ends in death is tolerable only if I'm doing something to affirm the life and defy the death—to cheat it, beat it back. For me this means making something new, imposing order, seeking meaning.

I am an arrow, pause never, leap forward always. By clear water, tongue swollen, press on; hungry, by tables of food, fly onward; lonely, by dancing girls, see only the winter ahead. Never do I look at a thing and see that thing, but look into a thing and ask what is it for? to what does it lead? And what I find, always, is string of the bow. The archer is a madman and blind.

The goad is in me, makes agitation, eventually hope. I locate the goal somewhere else, pursue it there. I'm off. The wheel spins: religion, Marxism, science, philosophy, medicine, now psychoanalysis.

Psychoanalytic truth is . . . what? Many things. It's a formal coherence of theory. It is also a certain correspondence between theory and behavior, and hence a predictive truth—though that's very shaky. It's that story of Simon's. It's Freud's assertion that no event of inner life could be other than it is, that nothing of soul escapes the deterministic net, that the fleeting wordless images are in principle reducible to formula and, though infinitely more complex, are no less lawful than the movement of planets, that free will is but a subjective state to be causally explained like any other. There is also in psychoanalysis a rough-and-tumble therapeutic truth: patients do get better. And an interpretive truth: it throws light in some shadowed corners. I work hard, master these truths, but the elusive anguish remains. It's the preoccupying concern, overrides everything else; and I discover that the whole point of searching out truth, psychoanalytic or otherwise, is to fight it. What won't help—and nothing will!—has no importance. The truths are still true but meaningless, mock me with impotent validity.

That was a shrewd guess of Simon's—but that's all. Most analysts would allow that the evidence did not warrant the prediction, that many unreckoned and unmeasured variables may have brought about (or might have prevented) the outcome. Analysts are modest this way; "We need more evidence," they say, thereby cloaking a Promethean arrogance. For the assumption implicit in Simon's story— one which most analysts would share—is this: that there are general laws of mental functioning (repetition compulsion, transference and displacement, et cetera) that, together with a sufficiently exact and extensive knowledge of initial and intervening conditions (traumatic event, reactivation in free association, and so on) make possible, in principle at least, the prediction of future mental events.

I used to be fluent at this game, facile in reducing a man to psychodynamics; now am silent, can't bring myself to mouth the clichés. Yet it was just this arrogance of psychoanalysis that drew me to it in the first place. For, acting with the conviction of freedom and choice, I would see later, that I had been driven and so came in time to the sense of being lived by unknown forces. Psychoanalysis promises insight into this darkness, and, through insight, control. Determinism thus ministers to the quest for certainty; it asserts regularity, denies any fundamental chance or chaos. For the lost security of God in the heavens it substitutes an immutable orderliness, not only in heaven but also on earth, in the mind of man and in the heart of the atom—to which Einstein gave voice in his vehement disavowal of chance: *Der Herrgott würfelt nicht!* ("The Lord God does not throw dice!")

Yet the history of determinism is a history of paradox—and this, itself is a paradox, since the whole point of determinism is the deletion of inconsistency. Religious determinism runs a veritable gauntlet of paradox: a wholly good God creating a world marked by evil; man being free to choose, yet God having foreknowledge; God being omnipotent, yet man being responsible. Nor is scientific determinism much better off. All is well when we deal with isolated systems, such as our group of planets, which we can observe and measure without disturbing. This is the determinism of Laplace: the demon stands outside the system on which it makes pronouncements. But so soon as we say "All is determined," and really mean *all*, we're in trouble; for we're talking about a system which includes ourselves and our talking—like the map of an area which includes a map of that area—and every word we utter is a change in that which the word is trying to pin down.

No one could have been more explicit or passionate

143

than Freud in insisting that every last wisp and shred of psychic occurrence is rigidly determined; yet it was Freud who found it necessary to say that the object of analysis is "to give the patient's ego *freedom* [his italics] to choose one way or the other." We, as psychoanalysts, expose to a patient why he *has* to be the way he is, then expect him to use this insight to become different from the way we have proved to him he can't help being. We try to climb out of this pit by asserting that causes effecting character change operate not only in childhood but throughout life, that the interpretations of an analyst are one class of such causes, and that these may relieve a neurosis in the same deterministic way that certain other causes produced the neurosis in the first place. The hope of radical change, we say, calls, not for the suspension of exceptionless determinism, but just the opposite—for a more vigorous application of the deterministic principle. Then we're really in trouble; for we're appealing for support for a law which, we say, cannot conceivably be disobeyed and hence needs no support. Here, without awareness, we invoke our double standard: expressly declaring our patients to be determined, we covertly regard ourselves as being free. Otherwise we should have to admit that our interpretations are just as incapable of being anything other than what they have been, are, and will be, as the phenomena to which they are addressed.

There is no escape from this impasse, and it has come to explicit formulation by Gödel and Bridgman: A system dealing with itself encounters paradox; its postulates cannot be verified within the system. A deterministic psycho-analyst is like the Cretan passionately declaring all Cretans to be liars; like the barber, instructed to shave all men who do not shave themselves, wondering what to do about his own beard. As psychoanalysts our voices are getting hoarse, our beards are growing longer, and we are getting no wiser.

But one can't keep walking away from one illusion into another. I see the pattern now, and with analysis I stick, and work; and gradually elaborate a criticism, giving up as little as possible. My disillusion, I decide, is not with the science of psychoanalysis but with its dearth of science. Too many unverifiable intuitions, too many glib explanations. Anybody who can learn to say "the opposite may also be true" can get to be an analyst. No search for a crucial experiment that might falsify our suppositions.

The wrath of disillusion is thus focused on one small outpost of science, and science itself goes scot free. Psycho-analysis is scapegoated, but intelligence is not impugned. I'm able to retain the crucial assumption: that there's no better way to approach any problem than the way of intelligence. The source of illusion and failure—the source, ultimately, of that inner pain—is in ignorance and dogma; the locus of value is inquiry. The urgency is to have the freedom to see what is there to be seen.

This is the last stand of a rational man. From this position there can be no retreat. Lose this and the war's over. It is also the strongest stand, for it lays claim to so little. Consider what assaults can be thrown back. A hundred thousand people die in Hiroshima: a great crime, to be sure, but not to be laid at the door of science. The evil issues from institutional anachronisms, such as the national state, which misuse the creations of science; with the further progress of knowledge in all areas of experience, such barbarism will give way. In this position I can survive, unthreatened, the despair of Marxist, Christian, mystic—even the most able and dedicated—for I can, in each case, say, "He gave his allegiance to a value which, however disguised, claims to be absolute. Such a value places itself beyond revision, is institutionalized, defended as dogma, becomes an incubus on man, and finally falls. Such disillusion is inevitable for the seekers after certainty. But I, the illusionless man, an immune. I have no platform, hold no value beyond change, believe only in intelligent inquiry."

So I thought. Now I think this too will fall. Has fallen, I suppose. It's still true, perhaps, but that's not enough. For this position—like all the previous ones—is attempting, not just to be true but to diminish the elusive inner trouble. I can't believe it any more. This malady is beyond the reach of anything. What I ascribe to intelligence is true, but this truth, too, has become irrelevant.

So what to do? What *is* a rational man to do—having lost faith in reason? The question trips itself. I don't suppose it matters. I keep on working—not with hope, not with justification, but as a matter of taste. What else is there? Passivity, suicide, fleshpots. . . . I like the dignity of work. It has at least the merit of defiance, of shaking a fist at the heavens. But that's just whimsy. Make a value out of that, and it too will disappear.

I do not suppose this view to be general, but I know it to be common. It's easy to hide; and because of guilt (for it *is* a rejection of life and one *does* feel guilty) one wants to hide it. Young lovers close their eyes, old lovers dissemble. Does my wife know? I look at her face and remember the storm of our coming together. I was the rock and she the wave breaking over me—tossed, scattered, falling, but re-forming, coming always toward me, exploding, dismembered, thrown in a thousand directions, yet coming always back, rising with undiminished force and wholeness, enveloping me, until foam proves harder than granite, and sharpness is smoothed by green caress. This turning away from life betrays that love. I try to keep it from her, and she—since she cannot help—tries not to know.

What I speak of here is experienced by others in different ways: a sense of futility, an intimation of unimportance attaching to creative effort, a vague feeling that the author of any serious endeavor is fooling himself. Most common now is the bomb which lights the world with transience, shows us solid marble as papier-mâché.

My friend Jeff, sitting nearby, sees it as death. He too is an analyst, once a creative one, wrote a few brilliant papers . . . then silence. "I began to feel the black hand coming closer," he told me once, "the utter unacceptability, the inner shriek. People don't think about death. They go about their business, months pass; it rarely comes to mind. This is mental health. The self-righteous even call it courage. Psychiatrists affirm it; the denial insinuates itself even into the definition of normality. To be concerned with death, we say, is morbid. It's not true: the fear and the revulsion are universal, but ignored. The whole of civilization connives with this denial. All of the temples and bridges and novels and sonnets, all of the pyramids and paintings and symphonies and machines, all of the uses of reason, the clear concept, the unifying theory. These things are made with our life blood, with the days of our years. And who has it to spare? Why, men who will never die. So—obviously—those who do these things are not about to die. Well, . . . I *am.* So I no longer have the time."

And this sunny company, prosperous all, well-dressed, educated, cultured—blessed and fortunate, one might think, beyond all others—the cancer grows here too. I'm a clinician of despair, I know the little signs: the wordless shadow in the eye, the furtive pain around the mouth; and the thousand ways of denying it, rationalizing it, running away from it: the distraction with *things,* the attempt to bribe one's bitterness with luxuries (cars, houses, fur coats, country places); the flight into hobbies (sailing, chess, tennis, wine, poker); the weekends in Las Vegas and Acapulco; and the final common pathway of sex. We—all of us—go to cocktail parties, smile and talk and talk, we take care of children, and work, and take pride in what we do, and believe the trouble isn't there. But we fool ourselves. It's there, and we know it at night when the wind blows. And it's there, too, after analysis; for when you have been completely analyzed—whatever that may mean—when, at the end of the last hour of your, perhaps, third analysis, you shake hands with your analyst and leave his office for the last time—at just that moment you hear a song, a snatch of melody from the radio of a passing convertible, feel again the pressure of a girl's head on your shoulder when you danced with her to that song, years ago . . . the fumbling tenderness comes back and you feel an ache of longing . . . for something—not the girl, something else —something which has no name, lies beyond your grasp, and you know that analysis, however fine its net, could not capture this elusive anguish.

I observe Jeff again: slender and wiry, narrow face with something of the fox, cheeks hollow, brown hair, thin brown mustache, direct gaze, facile smile; his arm around a woman of rosy complexion, as if faintly blushing, soft red lips, and hair like a luminous cloud. Jeff's manner is serene, his gestures elegant, his dress impeccable. When he stands he is exemplarily erect, walks as though with pleasure at putting his feet on the ground. He reclines now in voluptuous relaxation, lights a cigarette, inhales deeply. A few years ago he was divorced, has not remarried; but seems happy, is much sought after for parties. Professionally he is prominent, speaks well, holds office, is in demand as a consultant.

He talks to me frankly on occasion, partly to taunt me, I

think; for once, having been his analyst, I was the focus of those hopes he now regards as illusions.

"I came to realize," he told me one day, "that I was no happier than my patients. They're so fortunate, these patients of analysts—money, intelligence, good health, good looks many of them—and so enslaved! A phobia holds them to one town, even one room. They're afraid of planes and don't travel, have social anxieties and avoid strangers. Always some kind of fear—of incest, of guilt feelings, of the strength of impulse, of experience . . . of life itself. And I too. A prisoner of my work as they of their neuroses. Gradually conviction fled my work. It happened on the quiet; for a long time I didn't notice. Then one day I took stock and found . . . nothing. I wasn't having fun; there wasn't time. I didn't make any money, was doing research. And why? To figure out more intricate psychodynamics, to spin out more theories, to publish more papers, to bind the contingencies of life. Nets to catch the wind. This wasn't what I wanted."

On another occasion he said, "People are afraid of pulse and change. Nothing stays the same. Always there's something new, and this is the best of life, but they hate it, cling, and want promises. 'Stay with me forever, forsaking all others.' They're trying to freeze the flow of life, want a relationship that won't move, and so they get trapped. The one who clings and the one who is clung to—both lose freedom. A man cowers in a dead marriage, afraid to leave a woman he no longer loves, but leers at every cute behind that waggles by. Nothing more common. But if you choose freedom you have to lose the person who has chosen security, because she—it's always a woman—has to have promises. Women hate freedom. They're never satisfied with life till they make it like death. So the price of freedom is loneliness."

Jeff will not build, has no trust in tomorrow, will give up no part of the present for the future. At the end of each day he collects his wage—youth, talent, time—and spends it all that very evening in calm and deliberate profligacy. Is this the way to live? The blond woman leans against him, her lips at his ear, her breast against his shoulder, and I feel the pinch of one life, want it both ways.

If you serve an ideal you lose the actual; if you cling to the actual, you lose sight of the ideal. You have a choice—character sets limits, I oversimplify—but you can't choose both. And you have to cling to something. So cling to the girl on the knee, Jeff would say, not the angel in heaven.

The ideal doesn't *mean* to take one away from life, but just the opposite, to lay hold of the best in life. It says in effect, "This is what's most precious. Cling to it at the expense of the rest." And that's the point—the expense. Because experience is not of a piece, and to cling to the ideal means to turn away from all in life that opposes it. And that's all right so long as the ideal is intact. We can lose a lot and keep going. But then the ideal slips away, we lose belief; that's what happens these days, and then we see where we are. Only then. We've been led away from the market place into the desert and there abandoned, provisionless, by our guide. Then we have to find the way back, and quick. When values collapse we have to refind the life process whence the values came: the market place, the feel and smell and taste of the actual, or we die.

Jeff's strength is his loyalty to the present. He won't wander. But I will, can't help it, am driven to make distinctions. I stagger back, get a good meal, and the idealizing starts all over. Life is so multiple, the flow of experience so bewildering, so contradictory, I begin to say, "This is better than that." And then, watch out! I'm on my way again. A guide beckons—a maiden with a veiled face and a hunger for promises—and I follow. Out in the desert she leads me and there vanishes like a mirage.

Yet so much there is of good, and of such pleasure: iced tea in summer in the south when one is a boy, the glass clouding purple, lemon gleaming yellow, and the thrilling coldness, the pungent sweetness; swimming at La Jolla in crystal water with the kelp waving and those bright fish flashing by; and this quintet of Boccherini, and books that catch your heart and sweep you into the lives of others; and friendship and the love of woman . . . and so much more. But still a bondage; for all this goodness, pleasure, is our mandate; in its pursuit is our compliance.

There are rebels among us, of a kind; I see two here. Martin von Haffner, wealthy, aristocratic, defending Communists in defiance of class and of state. And Amory Stone, golf pro, despite scandal, the anger of husbands, and the shrill and never still tongue of his thin embittered wife of nineteen married years, forever sliding hungry hands up the trembling thighs of other men's wives—"Every golfer," he says, "needs a hobby!" Skirmishes at the surface, defiance only of convention; to the twisted law of neurosis, compliance—the obedient living out of hatred of a father in the one, of quest for a mother in the other, and of God knows what else in both, but compliance nevertheless—just the ways they happen to dance to the piper who jigs us all. No rebellion here, but meekness; like singing "Nearer My God to Thee" as the *Titanic* goes down, like the pacific processions at Auschwitz, and, oh, the wild tearing sadness that we too, sentenced to die and well on our way, should move with such patience, such kindly grace and decorum, as this fine company seated here in orderly rows with tranquil upturned faces—charabanc to the churchyard.

Is there then no rebellion? The mandate of life is to live—to avoid death, to enlarge life, to live as well, as fully, according to our natures, as we can, for as long as possibly can be contrived. The only real rebellion then would be the sacrifice of life: not to cling and hang on and hold back, as we are ordered, but to give it up by choice. This is our only glove to throw in the face of existence. Not suicide, not the neurotic act, for that too is compelled; but to part with life freely, without sickness. How? To value something more than life—what?—some part of living more than the whole of one's individual life. Something, something . . . the creation of music, the discovery of truth, the loving of others—to die for such by choice, *that's* what I would do. To declare a love of life, and to give

allegiance to it, by creating something which would enlarge the lives of all, at the same time defying the sentence
of death by giving up one's life, precisely to achieve this
creation, before it is called for—that's what I want. Give
me an image!

A village square, a fountain, a spray of water pulsing in
the wind; sunlight and a streamer of rainbow, and around
the square the life of the village: the few—exploiters, ma-
nipulators, parasites—who serve only themselves, and the
many who serve others while serving themselves; the
mother caring for her child, the doctor tending the sick,
the baker baking, the housewife cleaning, the psychoanalyst analyzing; children rolling hoops in the street, young
people swimming and lying in the sun, everywhere the
pursuit of the fullness of life; in a shuttered room the architect seducing the doctor's wife, while from the tavern
comes a polka and the splash of beer, and under the plane
tree old men playing chess. But one there is who does none
of these things, who sits at the fountain dreaming, watching in the spray of water, curtained by wind and jeweled
by sun, a pulsing flag only he can see and none but him
will follow, who will die young, having traded a part of
life for the making of beauty. This is the real defiance;
this is what I would do.

But I have tried and failed. I feel, at the mere thought, a
sick aversion. I have no knack, can find no path, would fail
again. Begin to act—even at random—and you begin to
hope. Begin to hope and you will perceive your action
makes sense, that it keeps the ship afloat and on a steady

154

course, that you will come to a safe harbor rather than a bad end. Is it only by not acting one gives up illusion? Can it be this hard for all who create? And is this really a wish to give something, or a disguise for the wish to get? to wrest something from the world? fame perhaps? How be sure? This doubt can impugn every motive, halt every action, insure that I do nothing, ever. What is it I lack— talent or courage? This is all in darkness.

Anyway, even should I succeed, might it not still be a dance to an unheard tune? to me an improvisation, but to the puppeteer, moving me on unseen threads, just a routine? The poet in the square may be acting out a given destiny, however obscure, as surely as the rest of us—to my eyes rebellion, to some higher vision compliance. Might it not in fact already have been determined that I go through this argument with myself today, that I struggle in just this way toward a decision that, unknown to me, is foregone? What is the issue? To try to create something of value . . . or to hell with it! But is this a decision I'm *going* to make—or one already made for me by complex and immeasurable causes, fixed within me as an unveering potentiality, to be revealed in time in the illusion of will?

I don't know. Can one know such a thing? Would it make a difference?

Perhaps a great difference; for if the issue is already settled I shall lose interest—do now lose interest even at the thought—even without knowing which way it has been settled. This kind of thinking is work—or the illusion of work, which is just as hard, and, being useless, is worse—

and I'll not do it for nothing. If I regard myself as a puppet, I'll forget the whole problem, will give myself over to
the enjoyment of the music, will attend to the grace of my
wife's ankle, her sweet sensuous mouth, will try to live
with more style; for if a life can leave no residue of value
then the performance is all. What a good life this is with
the love of this woman, with health, and the sun coming
up every morning. A thousand blessings and no cause for
complaints, and why am I spoiling a marvelous afternoon?
Who could have more cause to be happy?

In this way would I dismiss a morbid mood . . . or
would try. And if this didn't work I'd turn on it the tools
of my trade, would invoke from childhood the faded image
of an implacable father, restate the error of his ways with
me, affirm the sense of guilt he must have instilled, then
aim the old interpretation: This restlessness, this nagging
wish to create, this view of life as a procession to the grave,
all this is but the compulsion to expiate a fantasied murder. And if the melancholy still would not yield I might
take myself for further analysis to another of my own kind,
to a master mechanic of mind, inviting him to treat me as a
mechanism, asking him not for suspension of causality in
psychological affairs but for new links in the causal chain,
interpretations to divert the outcome—quite ignoring the
curious paradox (he being as much a puppet as I, his interpretations as fully determined as my ailment, and my
very going to him as unavoidable as his responding in his
particular ways) that nothing new could occur, only the
mechanical unfolding of what was there all along and in-

evitable.

If, however, I should take the view that what I shall decide is still open—not just unknown but really open, not fixed by antecedents, unpredictable at this point by any intelligence however superior, even by Laplace's omniscient demon—I would incline to continue the struggle, to anguish over it, try to think it out, find my way. Because the decision would be mine, something made, a creation.

So it does make a difference and I must take a stand. What have I—choice or the illusion of choice? That intention may determine action is not in question; but what of intention? Is it but a proximate cause, itself the effect of preceding causes, extending in iron-locked linkage backward in time, ramifying, unbroken, endless? Or may will create something new, something not possibly to have been predicted from any prior state? Freedom, if it exists, has limits: I have such a body as this, I bleed; have two eyes not ten, live at 98° not 120°, am impelled by drives, sexual, aggressive; eventually will die. But within these limits what am I—free or simply unaware of the strings that move me? Is this something that can be reasoned out? What is determined is predictable—if one knows the general laws and the initial and intervening conditions. If everything is determined, so also must be this issue I'm grappling with —to create or not to care. Could this decision, to my knowledge unmade as yet, be at this moment, under any conceivable circumstances, predicted?

Not possible, I think, not even in principle, not even if I knew all—all events, all forces, all impingements that had bearing, inner and outer, past and present, in measured quanta, infinite ramification . . . not even then. For the predicting would itself inject something new, itself a cause; and there would be no getting around it, not even if I could take this new cause into account, weigh it, foresee its effects near and far—not even then; for just this "taking into account" would again deflect my aim. Nor could anyone else, however fully informed, predict for me; for his observings would alter the observed in unmeasurable ways. Always there is something left over, always the future eludes us.

In viewing neuroses Freud tried to achieve the detachment of a scientist in a laboratory working with a specimen, himself uninvolved. On this model it was logically tenable to regard events within the supposedly isolated psychic apparatus of the patient as determined. Over the years, however, the therapist has increasingly been recognized as participant and involved—whether he wants to be or not, whether he knows it or not. Events in the therapeutic process occur in a field which includes him as well as his patient. On this model the deterministic view entails paradox and becomes untenable.

This development parallels the increasing recognition in all sciences that the object of knowledge is not to be separated from the instrument of knowledge, that there is no such thing, as Bridgman puts it, as a "naked object." Psychoanalysts generally refer to the Uncertainty Principle only by way of asserting that it is no threat to the deterministic view, that, though it is not possible to ascertain for small particles both position and velocity, such particles do of course *have* both, and some day with more delicate instruments both may be knowable. But this is precisely what the Uncertainty Principle contradicts, as the physicists have made unmistakably clear; and among the theoreticians Einstein, in upholding the fundamental orderliness of matter, seems on the minority side. Such disputes are not to be ruled on by an outsider, but what, at the very least, is beyond doubt is that determinism in psychology can expect no support from physics.

Exhilaration in this . . . and paradox. To view the world as determined, this has been man's courage, even impertinence, and his glory—an assumption most radical, inviting us to isolate segments of experience into closed systems, to discover their regularities, formulate their laws, and so to control the world; and we have: bridges and planes and hospitals and ships, and all of civilization bear witness. But to view ourselves—our visions, our very impertinence—as determined, this is an assumption most conservative, inviting us to conform to such laws of our nature as we may imagine. Can only imagine, never know, for we are involved; and can no more demonstrate than could we the laws of falling bodies in an atmosphere of random rifle fire. By assuming ourselves to be cogs in a mechanical universe, our lives the ticks of the great clock, we encourage ourselves—subtly, unwittingly—to act as we have always acted, to believe as we have always believed. Implicitly we, as psychoanalysts, encourage our patients to disparage will, to assume that nothing can be done until insight is complete. We postulate an indwelling essence that determines our lives, regard it as natural law; then come to feel (senselessly, for natural law is that which cannot be disobeyed) that we must act in accord with this essence, as if a break with the past were a breach of decorum, disagreeable, willful. Determinism leads us thus to label the leap as a sickness—Gauguin sailing for Tahiti is "acting out"—and in the very next breath to deny that it is a leap at all, to see it rather as consonant with concealed tendencies, indeed as the unavoidable product of neurotic conflict, even predictable. Not believing in freedom we become inattentive to the choices wherein it is manifest, assume we cannot reshape our lives, that a world state is impossible, that war is inevitable; and so it comes about that dreams are to be analyzed, that visions indicate psychosis—and freedom slips away.

Ortega y Gasset would have me believe that there is within me a destiny—a vocation in the largest sense of this word—which lies behind my "actual life like its mysterious root, as the hand lies behind the thrown dart," an "authentic I" which calls but does not compel: I may evade it, run from it, and so perjure my being, or may turn to it as my task, grapple toward its realization. This is Luther's "I can do no other," and I have had such moments. I know the feeling. Is this a guide?

But what—or who?—is this self to which I should be true? something innate, inscribed in origins and depths? I

find it inscribed only in past choices and their conse-
quences. Who am I?—why none other than he who chose
this work, took this wife, fathered these children, made
those countless commitments, and undertook those myriad
responsibilities in which my life is now webbed. The more
consistent these choices—with each other and with prior
choices—the more integrated the self they progressively
shape; the more integrated this self the more compelling
will be its demand that further choices accord with its values, coincide with its direction; and the further this process is extended, in time and in number of committing decisions, the stronger the self will become, the more nearly ir-
resistible its mandate, until it may at last defy any power
on earth and lead one to the stake rather than to recant.
This is the destiny that is character. And still nothing,
even so, can guarantee its rightness. There was no blue-
print, nothing prior to the free and therefore ultimately
arbitrary choices with which it was built. Its authenticity is
its wholeness.

Gauguin at thirty-five appeared the authentic banker;
only the break in his life reveals the split, the identity of
artist behind the role of banker. We say "role" of banker
because it's past, and we *know*, but how was it for Gauguin? How could he know what was structure and what
was façade? "Am I a banker with a hankering to paint, or
an artist hiding in a banker's life?" It would have been a
comfort to him to label his leaning as destiny, to "realize,"
as it were, that an unseen hand had set him on the trajectory of artist, but could he believe that? Can we?—when

the warring identities are themselves arbitrary, being but the result of two series of choices diverging now too far for one life to hold, and perhaps neither, if there *were* a destiny, meant for him? God's finger does not point: he made a leap, evicted the banker, gave the artist room to spread out, and so began a series of choices which created a self we think more authentic than the old—and so indeed it was if it fused into wholeness the passionate fragments of his nature. As Tahitian artist he disappears from our view, but it is only his death that makes that identity final. To live is to choose and so to continue to be shaped by choice, and a self hardened into final immutable shape is dead though its bearer may still breathe and move. Were Gauguin alive and making choices how could we know where they would carry him? Further in the same direction? Perhaps. But how be sure they would not again set his life on a different course, so creating a different self, even one as far surpassing in integration, and hence authenticity, the artist as the artist had surpassed the banker?

There is no help here. To be true to myself is no guide, for it means being true only to what I already am in whole or in part and so can lead to nothing new. To believe the task of my life to be already decided, like orders from headquarters which I as soldier must find and execute, . . . this is a turning away from the ultimate choice. The orders I'm most concerned with are those yet to be written, by me. Anxiety may lead me to disclaim creation, construe it as discovery, for much, even most, of life is necessity, but beyond constraint there lies in darkness a realm of freedom where there is no design until I make it. Here is the possibility of creation. Here the question is not Who am I? but Who shall I be? Who . . . ?

But might there not be, I must ask, an orderliness inaccessible to me, undemonstrable but invincible, of even the most tenuous events of dream and heart and thought, of these very questionings down to the last twist and comma, an orderliness such that—could one know all yet affect nothing—the future could be seen? such that, given the nineteenth century, the history of the twentieth could be written in full? such that, given in its entirety any instant in time, all future instants could be charted?

Along the wall move two columns of ants, one toward the winery, empty-handed, the other away from it with grain. Were it possible for one of these ants to consider this problem, what conclusions would his position in life make possible? That one there, for example, the big one, on his way to the winery but taking his time about it, turning around, standing up and looking about, stopping his returning colleagues, sniffing their burdens, lording it over them, tempted I think to snatch a grain, join the returning column, and so short-cut the trip. He would declare his freedom, I'm sure of it, would say he goes where he pleases, and find in his erratic excursions cogent proof. And should some scientist-ant—to press this analogy as far as possible—set about to prove him wrong, to portray his behavior as determined, this very effort might send the big one scurrying off the path, so, all the more conclusively, to establish his freedom. But I have a larger view and see a lawfulness unknown to him. He is constrained to this path; I know where he will go, when return, and with what burden. His freedom, if he feels it, is illusory.

And might there not exist somewhere a point of view as detached from me as mine from these ants? an intelligence as superior? to which every aspect of my life—including even this decision I've not yet "made"—is seen as an immutable sequence of cause and effect and hence predictable? How can I know? I can't, I suppose, nor can I dismiss it; I am given pause by the thought of an ant's denying *my* existence and of his never knowing the fatuousness of his error.

But what, if it should exist, would be the nature of such an intelligence? It could not be that of a man, for a man's observations would be interventions. It would have to be as far removed from us as we from the ants, as superior to us in knowledge and understanding, able to know and measure our most intimate vaporous fancies, including these very speculations, without affecting what was known and measured—in a word, God.

Suppose then I postulate God—simply as a vantage point for the observation of man as determined. Such a postulate cannot establish determinism in the affairs of men but makes the assumption logically tenable. But does not, I discover immediately, dispel the issue of freedom. For what about God's acts? God's thoughts? God's observations? Are they determined? If not determined, then there *does* exist something outside causality. If determined, then I must postulate a super-God in order to make sense of the assumption that God is not free.

Determinism, it appears, smuggles the idea of freedom past the custom officials of science. Laplace supposes that a demon, fully informed about every particle in the universe, could predict the future—and so, unnoticed, locates freedom with the demon, without whom the image is lost. Always we impute the existence of something, somewhere, which can act in a way that not even in principle could be predicted. For freedom is another word for life; without it there is nothing, not even determinism. If we think of the lawfulness of falling bodies we presuppose a human intelligence free to experiment, to measure the fall of iron and apples and feathers, in air and in vacuum and in windstorm. And if we shift attention to the creativity of the experimenter and regard that too as determined then, whether we know it or not, we locate freedom in a suprahuman experimenter. Determinism, declaring no exception, rests solidly on an exception. The idea of freedom is inalienable; if we deny it to ourselves we ascribe it to gods.

So, then, where locate it? There may indeed be a level of observation from which the life of man may be seen as determined; lack of evidence cannot prove its nonexistence. Likewise there may, beyond that, be an even higher level of observation from which events at the intermediate level would be predictable. One such, or two . . . or many. Or none. Here reason ends in choice: Our lives are determined and there is a God; or Our lives are free and man is God. There is no evidence here; both positions are logical, neither is subject to falsification.

Where lies my heart? Either way I may be wrong; so which error, I must ask, would I rather risk—to be an arrogant puppet who thinks he's a god or a humble god who thinks he's a puppet? For me the answer is clear, better to try for too much than too little; I elect to believe our future is unwritten, that we create it as we will.

But freedom is not fortuity, does not war with continuity, means only that we may make out of past and present something new, something which is not a mechanical unfolding and cannot have been foretold, that no law limits how far we may go, how wide, how deep. We are gods because we create.

And I? Tomorrow the sun will rise on the same routine, and what can all this mean? What can I create? Where is the poetry of which I am capable? Of what nature? Where can I. . . .

Applause and the conductor bowing, the audience to its feet with bravos, the orchestra standing . . . then an ending; the scraping of chairs, musicians beginning to leave the stage, the audience breaking up, people turning to each other . . . hello, hello, wasn't it simply marvelous . . . false smiles, ladies comparing dresses, jewelry, wrinkles, the color of hair, men comparing bosoms, hips, thighs, ankles; champagne around the swimming pool with talk of music and books, introductions to a vintner, a violist, and a critic; dinner on the terrace with four wines, introductions to a judge, an economist, and a college student, talk of delinquency and taxes and schools; then the long walk to the car, cool now with the sun dropping behind the fog bank, the winding road down the mountain, down, down, in darkening twilight, and finally the freeway (from the mountain an ant trail but here a whine and threat and roar of cars), a glare in the mirror of weaving lights separating into two streams to pass, the sharp licking sound of tires as the road gets wet in the dripping fog; then the flashing red lights and stopped cars and . . . yes, yes . . . the twisted metal, the broken glass, the smell of gasoline, and there by the road (my wife's fingernails biting my arm), a man on a heap of gravel as if on a bier, ashen face turned to the black sky; then beside him waiting for the ambulance . . . about twenty, I'd say, and now a fractured skull, and oh . . . how to live? how to live? and will this one get another chance? . . . nothing to do but hope and see that he breathes, and . . . how will he use it if he gets another chance? how ever can we find our way out of this murk? Then the siren, white sheets and stretcher, and he's gone, and I'm back in the car, wife trembling on my arm, and we go on, lost, in this night of blinding lights and confusing signs—and it has to be this way; we want it too easy, want a routine of creation, a paved road into the unknown, but darkness is our workshop, here creation begins . . . and still time to try.

THE
MORALIST

ALMOST A HUNDRED
YEARS SINCE NIETZSCHE
announced the death of God, since Ivan Karamazov declared that everything is permitted; and ever more clearly
we see a universe without transcendence, animated by
nothing beyond the likes of us—strange beings probably on
the planets of other stars, but no God—nothing up there
beyond the spiral nebula, no guiding principle, nothing to
give the law, to stand apart from the human adventure and
judge. Not that God has averted his face, it was a face in
our dreams; not that the universe is indifferent, it does not
perceive. Only we judge; and, having renounced ascrip-
tion to heaven, our judgments lack the authority of reaching us across great distances. As they have but the authority of ourselves, we know how fallible, arbitrary, even
shabby, they must be.

Yet a morality of sorts survives. Once we thought that,
without threat or promise of ulterior punishment and reward, man would run amuck. He may still, and if with
our new ways we should destroy the world a strong case

might then be made—were anyone left to make it—that restraint was lost with the discovery of permissiveness, that morality did not survive God. But we've got a chance apparently, and meanwhile decency is not lost; we hold ourselves in check, many of us, act more like men than beasts. Why?

"I could not bear to break my word or to kill," wrote Nietzsche. "I should languish, and eventually I should die as a result—that would be my fate." Why? He has already diagnosed such sentiment as the morality of slaves, germinating from the submissiveness into which they are beaten. Could he make no use of his insight? And whether he could or not, cannot we? If we agree with his findings can we not surmount the neurotic guilt imposed by a bourgeois morality, seize the freedom we have at last been able to formulate? "I became a traitor," writes Sartre, "and have remained one. Though I throw myself heart and soul into what I undertake, though I give myself up unreservedly to work, to anger, to friendship, I'll repudiate myself in a moment, I know I will, I want to. . . ." Yet in the very next breath he is saying, "I fulfill my commitments like anyone else. . . ." Why? Would he have us think it simply suits his inclination to do so—constantly, for a lifetime? Beyond belief! Why then, on what basis, does he deny the vagrant appetite which would violate commitments?

We're all Nietzsche, we're all Sartre, unbelievers, spinning wildly for a moment on our cinder through a silent universe, unnoticed, talking our heads off, nothing to cling to but ourselves—so what, then, is the nature of our surviving morality? What validity, if any, has it? And what basis, if any at all, have we for strictures against those who ignore it, who enter upon a license we deny ourselves?

Let us think.

When morals can no longer be validated above they must be validated below. By life—of which it may be said, at the very least, there isn't anything else. What serves life, enlarges and enriches it, is good; what destroys or diminishes it is bad. Is this the source and meaning of morals?

But what life is meant? Cannot be all life. We go out of our way to save skylarks and otters, condors and the sabertooth tiger, but as indulgence not sacrifice. When it's we or they we chose ourselves, waste no tears over cancer cells or tubercle bacilli, bugs on our windshield, or sheep in the slaughter house. So who is "we"? All mankind? But men tear at men: where else but here do we need a guide? Do I, as a German in 1934, acquiesce to the Third Reich, fight it from underground, or flee? Do I, as an American in 1966, support my country's stand in Vietnam, oppose it, or do nothing? And what about deprivation of the rights of Negroes? Do I shrug, fight, or send ten dollars to CORE? To stand above such conflict, holding hands with God, loving all men, is to dodge the question, walk out on the examination as if having wandered into the wrong classroom: "I didn't approve," said the German, "but what could I do? Anyway, I really didn't know what was going on."

Whose welfare is to be served by morals? Men of good will? But who is to point them out? I want to fight with the good guys, but many of the (to me) bad guys are themselves convinced of rightness, and though we Americans know that, while the Germans usually and the Russians always are bad guys, and the French and Italians take turns, *we* are always the good guys—are we not growing less sure?

We may remind ourselves that morals serve principles, not men, but that's no help; for principles, if they have not the authority of God, have the authority only of men, and men differ. The principles of *which* men? Moreover, even with agreement on principles there is conflict in application; armies destroy each other in the name of freedom.

Whose life, then, shall be served? In psychological terms the issue is identification: how wide, how narrow is the range of empathy? how far does it reach into alien land? what determines its expansion and contraction? But morality is imperative, not descriptive; psychology restates but does not solve. The question remains: What is to be the field, the extent, of identifications? All one's friends? All white people? All Americans?

There is a point of view which holds that the test of right conduct can be, interchangeably, one's own good or the good of society, for the reason that in the long run they tend to coincide. Don't anguish over these alternatives, this view would say. Seeming opposition masks a hidden unity. Forget this soul-searching; be practical; come down from the metaphysical mists or you'll lose your way and end a martyr and absurd. The good life is simple: Follow your own interests with intelligence—with due regard for the rights of others—and be assured you serve the good of all. What's good for General Motors is good for the United States.

This is a view that deals with moral conflict by first denying its existence, then rationalizing self-interest. It's the ethics of money, of success, of generous social views and community responsibility, of contributions to CARE and Boys' Town and (increasingly with age and the hardening of arteries) to the Cancer Society and the Heart Association; it guards the sleep of men in mansions, in king-size beds, behind oak doors; is tailor-made for the likes of me. It is an ethic to justify a way of life already being lived, not one to question that way. Maybe what serves one and serves all do tend in the long run to coincide; but in the short run—which is where we live, where all our lives are spent—they clash and men die, and we must choose to intervene or to look away. A point of view that overlooks this choice, deaf to the din of this battle, is fine perhaps for the philosophic viewing-boxes of civilization where the strategy of progress is plotted in millennia but is no help to me. I'm on the field, I see what happens, and I know it's possible to do other than I'm doing.

My way of life looks good when viewed alone, questionable alongside the Christian way. Like the rich man of whom St. Matthew speaks, I am of good will and generous acts, have kept all the Commandments, so what lack I yet?

" '. . . go and sell that thou hast, and give to the poor
. . . and come and follow me.' But when the young man
heard that saying, he went away sorrowful: for he had
great possessions." I am he and have been going away sorrowful all my life, haunted by an admonition which allows
me comfort or virtue, but not both. My possessions are not
so great, but we are, each of us, rich in having a life to give
or withhold. The ideal of sacrifice is clear as day: it asserts
conflict between my good and the good of all and calls for
the giving up of my life for others. If you don't see any
such need or conflict, it would add, just pick up a newspaper, and it will hit you in the face.

A young physician was killed recently in Africa. He
could have treated the sick in St. Louis or New York; but,
as these places already have some medical care even for the
poorest, he took his skill where the need was greatest,
which happened to be a dangerous place. He was unarmed,
represented no government, taught no religion, sought no
publicity; he was treating the sick. He was half my age, his
profession is mine; but I have elected to practice this skill
in San Francisco. Am I entitled to regard myself and him
as morally equal? How about it? Congo, Zanzibar, Califor-
nia, what's the difference? People get sick everywhere, rich
men and poor, civilized and savage. Somebody has to treat
the neurotics of this jeweled promontory, and if I choose
this task and this place am I not, as much as he, in the service of mankind? He was more adventurous, perhaps, had a
different style, liked to travel; but we are brothers, we
treat the sick—he and I and the Park Avenue surgeon.

Is this not credible? I could make a stronger case, I'm not really trying because I don't believe it. My way of life and the way of my young colleague are at variance. My way, whether admitted or not, exemplifies the position that the good is what is *both* good for others and good for me; the way of my colleague, now rotting in Africa, that the good is what is good for others even if bad for me, even if it cost my life. We shall not add to the dignity of language if we use it to obscure this difference.

But for what motive might I elect to serve others at such cost to myself? If it were God's will and I wanted to please him or feared his anger, there would be a reason. Christ promised the rich man treasure in heaven, but not me; Christ and his Father and heaven have disappeared and no getting them back. Nobody promises me anything, and this life right now—the sacrifice of which is under consideration—is all there is.

So what else? What could motivate sacrifice? What honor beckon? What fear spur? . . . Nothing. Continuing on the old path I have nothing to fear. No one criticizes, no one shames; honors fall upon me. Could I perhaps do it without reason, without motive, simply from wanting to? Sure. And if my aunt had wheels she'd be an omnibus. It happens I *don't* want to; if I did I would do it. It is easier, more comfortable, and much safer to stay here and do what I've been doing. That, obviously, is what I want, and I'll not exchange a way of ease for a way of sacrifice unless I come to feel I ought, am bound to, must. And what could bring me to that?

If nothing impels me to sacrifice, perhaps nothing restrains me from license. Consider my friend Jeff—becoming more and more self-centered as he grows older, yet so charming, urbane, intelligent that he is loved all the more. His psychiatric research is a thing of the past, his clinical dedication but an elegant posture, and right now . . . ten o'clock in the evening . . . he is probably having dinner at Trader Vic's with an old wine and a young female, savoring the former, enticing the latter, plying her with profundities and wit, then to the Fairmont for another drink and some dancing, and on to his flat high on Telegraph Hill where he will roll her in bed with an orgiastic view of the ships and the bay and both bridges. Is this the way to live? . . . It's not for me, I think, however much I envy it. Instinctively I feel it's wrong.

Yet this reaction must be disallowed. Instinct affirms the past and calls for reënactment, gives voice to what I am, knows not of what I should be, speaks my prejudices, finds reasons, enunciates my stops where self-seeking is halted by guilt. It tells me what's fit and proper, but tells another, with the same certainty, "niggers gotta be kep' in their place." It would be a miracle and incredible if my stops—acquired as they were from all the random genetic and experiential dice-throwing that goes into the making of character—had authority transcending my circumstances. I can't believe it. My stops rationalize the position I'm in, cannot judge it. Like an automatic pilot they keep me going in the same direction, at the same speed and altitude; they correct deviations but do not validate my destination. The aircraft is steady, on course due west, weather clear as can be expected; engines okay, not like new but reliable still for quite a while. Everything is in order, I am the captain and have time now to walk around, observe the airship, look at maps, and to realize that the course, however steady, was a random fall. No one waits. Strange that a machine so delicate and complicated, proceeding on so costly a flight, should have no dispatcher, no mission. But that's the way things are. I happen to be going this way, and that's all. I could change, and may ask, equally, Why should I? and, Why should I not? Is there then no way to judge ends? no escape from arbitrariness?

The trouble, perhaps, is that we can reason about ends only by viewing them as means to more distant ends, while morality, by its nature, is final. An honest man whose honesty derives from his reasoning that honesty is more profitable than deception presents us with strategy, not morals. We can be reasonable, it seems, only in the pursuit of something set by unreason, by passion, prejudice, chance; intelligence without limits, like mathematics without content, is sterile.

Now here's a paradox: no problem more urgent than morals, yet when, trying to deal with it, we seize complete freedom for the exercise of our problem-solving faculty, that faculty suddenly is impotent. Like a lever free of its fulcrum, it moves nothing. The old fulcra were the Ten Commandments, the Gospel of Christ, the Natural Order —all with capital letters. In the past we would discredit one absolute only to replace it with another; now we have thrown out the whole kit and caboodle and find that intelligence, lacking a fixed point, has no force at all.

But why must morals be embodied in a final end? Perhaps we must accept now that they are instrumental, the end being life itself. Perhaps the life process, which is all we have, must now become the fixed point, the ulterior consideration on the basis of which reasoning about morals will become possible. What serves life is good, . . . but this is a circle. Whose life? Mine or my neighbor's?

But wait. Might not biology in some more basic sense still be the fulcrum? A kind of cellular intuition perhaps, a tropism for avoiding extremes? Might not the very moderateness of my moral position, midway between my narcissistic friend and the selfless missionary, reflect this basic strategy of conserving life?

I think not. Intellect without limits, though it may not create, can still criticize, and in this capacity can shoot holes through such an armor for the status quo. My position is moderate because I call it moderate, and for no other reason. I select two moral positions that are on either side of me, equidistant, and designate them as extremes; then, using them as referents, I take my bearings and find to my gratified surprise that I'm in the middle. That's how I come to be situated between Jeff and the missionary. But I could just as well have designated the missionary and Dag Hammerskjöld as the extremes, whereupon I would be far out in self-interest. Or, equally, I could have chosen Jeff and an embezzler, perhaps that cool young man who took a million from an Oakland bank last month and disappeared into South America. No, . . . that's too risky: rather, Jeff and one of the robber barons who steal legally. In relation to them I would be far out in the direction of guilt, inhibition, and impoverished life.

The acceptance of moderation as the criterion of virtue yields no answer. For how possibly, if we ascribe no special merit to where we happen at the moment to be, can the moderate be known? We can know that where one is is the starting point of any journey, and moderation may be considered an attribute of process rather than location: any movement far or fast being radical, any movement slow or slight being moderate. But this is no help; for in which direction, I must then ask—at that cautious pace which defines moderation—should I proceed?

So what's wrong with narcissism? It's unfair to take without giving, to live for one's self when everything of value comes from others. But fairness is not the source of a moral rule but the rule itself, which is what is being questioned. What is the authority of fairness? Not the fairness that may be imposed, which may be dangerous to ignore, but the rule of fairness that one may or may not impose on one's own life. The rich man's son, for example, enjoying all the goods and services of the world—why should he be fair? If he doesn't produce something, it might be argued, all that he has may be taken away by revolution. But not in his time, he may suppose, and he may be right. What then? Perhaps the welfare of his own son or grandson might hinge on his present fairness? Yes, but why should this move him? Here again: good for whom?

The Illusionless Man

In a world of peril we huddle together, and from the proximity and coöperation of that huddle derives the identification of one's self with others, our tendency, in many circumstances, to think "we" not "I." Identifications may be narrow or wide, the extreme of narrowness being the opportunist whose boundaries of concern go no further than his skin, the extreme of breadth being the mystic who identifies not only with all life but with stones and stars, all that happens and all that is. At neither of these extremes can morality, which concerns the conflict of rights, exist. The opportunist, lacking identification with others, does not experience their rights as binding on him, hence deals with others in terms only of the opportunities and dangers they present. The mystic avoids the issue by so elevating and limiting his experience as to deal only with the unity behind, or below, the conflict: "Killing merely is one form of our wandering sadness . . ." wrote Rilke, embracing the universe. Most of us fall, between these extremes, in the land of morality. We identify ourselves, with an intensity inversely proportional to the psychological distance, with some considerable number of others—family, community, race, nation, religion, species—acknowledge their rights, and struggle with the conflict between theirs and ours. Differences in the character, the extent, and the intensity of identifications dictate our differing moral positions. Therefore, since identifications are ultimately to escape peril, morality may be seen as the distillate of security operations.

Now there's a view of things to take the grandeur out of

sacrifice. Victor and victim, the selfish and the serving, honest man and cheat—in motivation they're all the same. Christ and Pontius Pilate pursue in their differing ways the same goal. The missionary facing death to save a child, the psychopath with his *"Semper fidelis* to you, Bud! I've got mine, now you get yours," the driver who looks away from the accident, saying "I don't want to get involved," Rilke accepting everything, even the murder of innocents —all bear witness in the name of right and wrong only to the limitless variety of ways in which security, as mediated by identifications, may be conceived and pursued. But no reason to sneer. Having lost transcendent authorization, why not relocate morals, openly, on the ground of security?

. . . for whom? The old question is but transposed. A sharp and intelligent concern for the security of all will hardly dictate the same conduct as an equally sharp and intelligent concern for the security of one's self; the two are at odds, and morality can no more be validated by the conflict over which it presides than a court by its litigants. Believing as I do that a general war is the greatest collective peril, I might—were my motive the security of all—follow the path of Leo Szilard, create an organization for disarmament, write and lecture and campaign. This would mean the giving up of a comfortable, lucrative, and stable profession, and the taking on of a demanding, costly, and unstable life of planes and hotels and conference rooms, of failure too, most likely, and ridicule; yet such is as possible for me as it was for Szilard. If, however, the security of most concern to me is my own or my family's, I may simply go on as I am—perhaps giving a hundred dollars, instead of ten, to the World Federalists.

On second thought, I might give nothing, might simply drop the appeal in the wastebasket along with all the others. What's a hundred dollars, or ten, but a sop to my guilt for doing nothing? And why, if I freely elect my personal security as the referent of morals, should I feel guilty? Can't I do something about that?

My actual security, as it happens, has increased over the years, while those automatic promptings of conscience upon which depends the subjective sense of security have lagged, reflect still an earlier, more threatened, state. As an adolescent and young adult I was without place or purchase in society, alone, unskilled, always close to failure, rejection; and was prompted by such peril to far-reaching identifications, became what is called idealistic, strongly inclined to service, even sacrifice. Such insecurity, leading to such identifications, creating my particular moral principles, becoming automatically operative in conscience, controlling conduct with guilt . . . such is the chain of events which arrives now at the signing of checks for causes. But among the elements of the security I have gained—profession, property, reputation—is a skill particularly well suited to give some leverage with guilt. Not much, it's hard to change, but perhaps not impossible. If morality is indeed the distillate of security operations, and if I now elect—frankly, deliberately—to regard my individual security as the standard, and if that security is indeed much greater now than when my morality first crystalized —then what, if anything, could or should deter me from diminishing the extent and intensity of my identifications? of coming to live more for myself? of moving more in the direction of my friend Jeff?

Perhaps that man is social by nature. That even the most isolated of us lives in relatedness and interdependence. Alone in a locked room, despising men, one can't read a book or eat an apple without becoming indebted to countless of the despised; the room itself was hammered together by them. Man is the animal who remembers the past, preserves it, adds to it, passes it on. To be a man, by definition, means to share in this relatedness, to give to it as well as take from it; and maybe the only source of morality for godless men is the free choice to be a man rather than a beast. For to elect diminished relatedness and participation, less responsibility, narrowed identifications, is to move toward the jungle.

Yet this, too, begs the question. For these alternatives offer no choice, but rationalize an antecedent choice. "Man or beast" means "man or sub-man," which means "good or bad"; and to elect in this context to be a man means only to wish to be good, and that's admirable indeed but establishes no basis for morals. Evil, however we conceive it, pursues its course in the lives of countless men who want to be good.

So why, we must ask, must relatedness, however characteristic of man, be identified with good? Cows and coyotes huddle together too. Even if we should accept that man is social in essence and even if we accept that his biological and historical development has tended ever toward more relatedness, larger groupings, wider and stronger identifications—even then we have no ground for morals; for we are talking only of what is, or was, or will be, not of what should be. Teilhard de Chardin, extending into evolutionary time man's capacity for interrelatedness, foresaw the development of a universal mind, one all-embracing "envelope of thinking substance" covering the world. Let us grant this as a possibility but ask what reason have we for believing it good. Why should Teilhard's man of the future, lacking unique mind, be viewed as superman rather than sub-man? Why, given a choice, should we not elect Nietzsche's superman? Why not Jeff?

I have wider and stronger social identifications than Jeff, am more concerned with the welfare of others. Am I thereby superior? Not, I am sure, to his view. Even were he to grant that the difference between us is so marked and so significant that, if I be man, he must be non-man, even then . . . "Don't press me," he would say, smiling with characteristic affection and lightness, but in his thoughts he would say, "Very well, if you insist: of the two of us, *I* am the superman. Because more free, less guilty, more able to live. I don't think so much as you, nor probe morals, but I enjoy life more; and since from the vantage of the Horsehead Nebula in Orion neither you nor I nor anything we think matters a damn, pleasure is the only referent of value, and by that criterion I'm more advanced than you." And how is this gainsaid?

Not by force of logic. By leap of heart, if at all.

I am in the fast lane, in a drizzle of rain at dusk; ahead of me, at a safe distance, a gray Mercedes convertible; beyond the convertible a trailer truck. The brake lights of the truck go on; the Mercedes slows; I slow; then the truck speeds on; the brake lights go off on the Mercedes. I put my foot back on the accelerator—then suddenly the convertible is broadside; my foot hits the brake; the blurred horizon spins . . . fast . . . faster . . . raindrops coming toward my eyes, remembering wife, child . . . oh, darling! I'm so sorry! . . . expecting the crash . . . a wild tearing roar of tires, a fountain of gravel rising by the window, the car coming then to a stop, without impact, upright, on an embankment. The Mercedes is not ten feet away, miraculously undamaged, facing the wrong way in the slow lane, a young woman with brown hair stumbling out. I catch her by the shoulders, pull her off the roadway, hold her, trembling, as she twists back as if searching, making then an inarticulate sound of distress and pointing: in the fast lane is a dog, hindquarters crushed (by the truck probably, and that's why she tried to stop), struggling up on its forelegs, head straining upward, yelping feebly. I look up at four lanes of oncoming traffic—almost dark, faint streaks of rain slanting through the headlights—cars in the fast lane swerving outward to miss the dog, cars in the slow lane swerving inward to miss the Mercedes. The woman moves toward the road. "No," I say, "don't!" She twists toward me for a moment, her face frozen in horror and accusation, jerks away, runs for the road; hits me in the mouth as I catch her and pull her back, scratches at my eyes, screaming, "Coward! Coward! Let me go!" I pin her arms and we stand struggling in the rain, locked together, swaying, while the dog yelps; a car skids, a truck hits the dog, then a car with a thud, then another, and the dog is dead; the sirens then and flashing red lights and a police officer explaining that it's the fault of the dog's owner, who is liable, and who will be located from the tag on the dog's collar.

I could never have made it, I tell myself later, driving on alone. But what if it had been a child? I would have tried. . . . Would I? I have an image of my own child, lying there, of my running out to her, of being hit in the third lane just a moment before I would have been able to scoop her up. But I might just make it, not altogether hopeless; I would try; it would be unthinkable not to try.

But there *is* a child, I think, just not so close as that dog. So the woman is right, and I am a coward. And it seems to me that somewhere, at some forgotten corner, I made a wrong turn—away from the real world that had seemed to betray me, to look inward, to burrow ever more deeply within, coming to live with shadows, the real world lost to me now, no sureness in it, not even knowing where the fast lane is.

72 73 74 12 11 10 9 8 7 6 5 4 3 2